MRS. HARRINGTON DABBED HER eyes with her handkerchief, looked around, and then beckoned for the girls to come closer. "I am not supposed to tell anyone, but I don't think I can hold it in any longer. Precious is missing! Sh-sh-she's been, she's been—dognapped!" Mrs. Harrington's shoulders shook as she cried louder than ever.

"Dognapped! What do you mean? Someone's taken Precious?" asked Rosemary Rita. . . .

Mrs. Harrington reached into her bag and pulled out a folded piece of paper. . . .

The note read:

> *If you ever want to see your dog again, follow these directions. Put £500 and your pearl necklace in a bag. Put it in your trunk in the baggage room down the hall from your room.* DO NOT *tell the captain or the authorities. If you do, your dog is going overboard!*

The girls looked at each other in amazement. It was true. Precious had been dognapped!

Rosemary · at · Sea

When my grandmother gave me an hourglass for my **tenth birthday**, I had no idea how amazing it really was. With it, I can travel back in time and **visit my ancestors**! Each generation of my family has one girl named Rosemary, and each one saved her postcards and trinkets from the special moments of her life. Now, those postcards are my **passport to adventure**! You can come along for the ride with the *Hourglass Adventures* books.

The adventure doesn't have to end when you finish the story! Visit my room at **winslowpress.com**, and you can check out fun facts, master games, send **cool coded messages** and cards to your friends, or just surf around and see what's new. You'll find quizzes, **craft ideas and recipes**, new mysteries, and great links all over the Web—your imagination is the only limit!
The Hourglass Adventures #4
Rosemary
AND T
The Hourglass
Rosemary
AT
Barbara
The Hourglass Adventures #1
Rosemary
MEETS
Rosemarie
Berlin in 1870
Barbara Robertson
glass Adventures #2
Paris
Back to 1889
Barbara Robertson

www.winslowpress.com

Read about the *Hourglass*...

In the *Hourglass Adventures* books, Rosemary Rita travels to amazing places and times. Online, you get to do the traveling with games, activities, interactive mysteries, and more. Throughout this story you'll find online activity prompts at the tops of the pages.

Costume Shop:
Dress up Rosemary Rita at winslo

another
them

ano
then
owne
Preciou
"Hell
friend and
seems to like yo
my girl has a boyfrie   must
get them together to play."

"Mrs. Harrington, I'm surprised to see you up here. I thought you would stay on the Upper Deck," said Rosemary Rita.

"Well, dear, I wanted my Precious to get a little direct sunlight, although I must say it is windy here. Then again, I'm a sturdy sort. As I always say, a little fresh air never hurt anyone." Mrs. Harrington chuckled as she spoke.

Precious and Snowball nuzzled up close to each other. Rosemary Rita introduced May-May to Mrs. Harrington. Then they all sat down on deck chairs. Mrs. Harrington pulled a red ball out of her coat pocket and tossed it to Precious. The dogs nudged the ball back and forth to each other.

56 · THE HOURGLASS ADVENTURES

come up here. People are having too much fun for her taste. Besides, she doesn't think the cabins in second and third class are as comfortable. The Upper Deck is quite posh, you know."

"Oh, I think Gracie would like it here. She's so adventurous—"

"Gracie! You know my mother? And you call her Gracie?" May-May's eyebrows rose in disbelief.

"No, of course I don't know her. It's just that, um, James, well, he always refers to his Aunt Gracie as so much fun and everything. I guess I just *feel* that I know her." Rosemary Rita stumbled over her words as she tried to cover her mistake.

"It's true, James does get along well with

ROSEMARY AT SEA · 57

Like what you see? Log onto **winslowpress.com** and you'll find Rosemary's Room, and all of the activities from this book. Click on the prompt from the page you're reading to play the game, solve the mystery, master the activity, and explore Rosemary Rita's world!

Click into your own adventure!

Visit the *Hourglass Adventures* Web site at winslowpress.com.
Click on the cover of the book that you want to explore.

Choose an activity from your book.

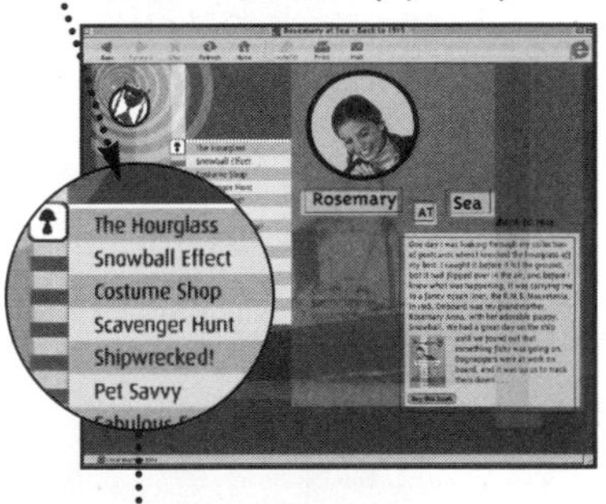

Check out all 16 Web activities in this book:

- Snowball Effect
- Costume Shop
- Scavenger Hunt
- Shipwrecked!
- Pet Savvy
- Fabulous Footwear
- Gingerbread House
- Difficult Decisions
- Cat or Canine?
- Say What?
- Muffin Madness
- Daring Detectives
- Ace Expressions
- Framed!
- Talk Back!
- What's Next?

Click

Rosemary · at · Sea

BY BARBARA ROBERTSON

Hourglass Adventures

Nº 3

ROSEMARY AT SEA

WINSLOW PRESS
NEW YORK

Library of Congress Cataloging-in-Publication Data
Robertson, Barbara (Barbara K.)
Rosemary at sea / by Barbara Robertson.—1st ed.
p.cm. — (The hourglass adventures ; #3)
Summary: Magically transported back in time to 1919, ten-year-old Rosemary Rita shares an adventure with her great-grandmother aboard the luxury ocean liner *Mauretania*.
ISBN 1-890817-57-0
[1. Time travel—fiction. 2. Magic—Fiction. 3. Mauretania (Ship)—Fiction. 4. Ocean liners—Fiction.] I. Title.

PZ7.R54466 Rg 2001
[Fic]—dc21
2001017693

Creative Director
Bretton Clark

Book Designer
Annemarie Cofer

Web site Designers
Annemarie Cofer
Patricia Espinosa

Web Programmer
John Fontana

Web site Content
Deirdre Langeland

PRINTED IN THE U.S.A
First edition, October 2001
2 4 6 8 10 9 7 5 3 1

WINSLOW PRESS
115 East 23rd Street, 10th Floor
New York, NY 10010

Discover *The Hourglass Adventures*' interactive Web site with worldwide links, games, activities, and more at winslowpress.com.

To **Ashley, Will,** and **Eileen**—

for making my **every day**

a wonderful adventure.

Rosemary · at · Sea

Chapter 1

THE · DOG · COLLAR · AND THE · POSTCARDS

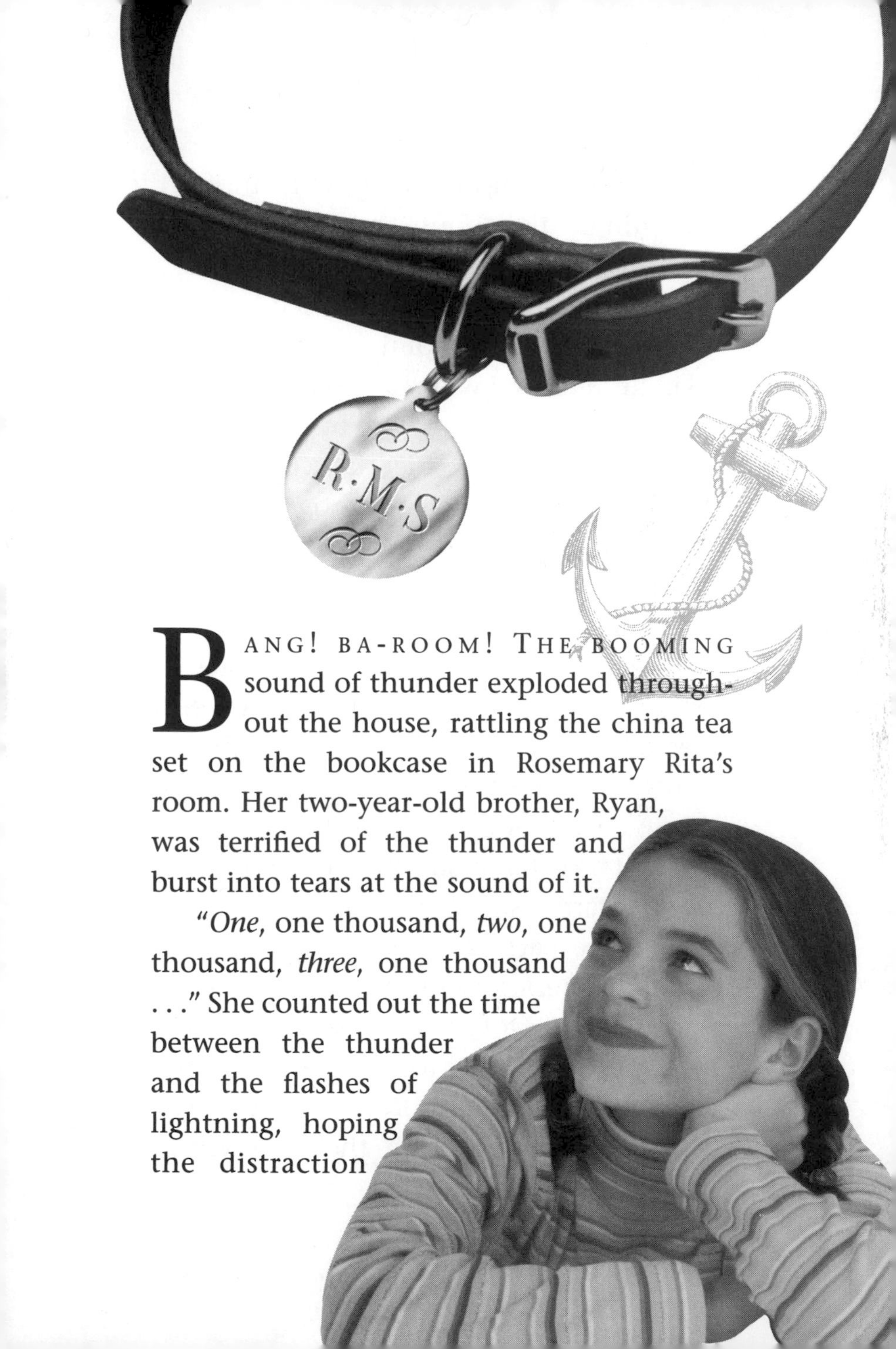

BANG! BA-ROOM! THE BOOMING sound of thunder exploded throughout the house, rattling the china tea set on the bookcase in Rosemary Rita's room. Her two-year-old brother, Ryan, was terrified of the thunder and burst into tears at the sound of it.

"*One,* one thousand, *two,* one thousand, *three,* one thousand . . ." She counted out the time between the thunder and the flashes of lightning, hoping the distraction might calm him down. "FLASH—there's the lightning! It's about three miles away," Rosemary Rita assured her brother.

"It gonna get me," Ryan cried.

"No, it won't, I promise. Let's go get your blankie, and Dad will read you a story before bed." She pulled him close to her.

BOOM! The thunder lashed out again. Ryan hugged Rosemary Rita tighter. She carried him to their dad, said good-night to both of them, and then walked back down the hall to her room. Gingerly climbing onto the mattress of her comfy four-poster bed, Rosemary Rita tucked her long legs beneath her. She was careful not to disturb the postcards that were stacked in neat piles on the white bedspread. She twirled a strand of her straight brown hair around one of her fingers as she started sifting through the postcards. They were part of a birthday gift from her grandmother, Rosemary, whom everyone called Mimi. Only two days ago, Mimi had sent her ten boxes for her tenth birthday. Since then, Rosemary Rita had spent nearly every minute exploring their contents. In addition to the postcards, the boxes were filled with special objects that had been collected by her grandmother and the other Rosemarys in the family who had come before her.

It was spring break from school and all her friends were away. Rosemary Rita had thought there would be nothing to do in Greenville. Boy, was she wrong! In the tenth box, Rosemary Rita had discovered a magic hourglass! When she held a postcard and flipped the hourglass over, she was transported back to the time and place connected with the postcard. Rosemary Rita had already been on two adventures and couldn't wait to go on another.

She fingered the dog collar that was lying on the bed next to the pile of postcards. It was made of brown leather and had a silver pendant engraved with the initials *RMS* hanging from the strap. Late yesterday afternoon, her brother Ryan had snuck into her room and removed the collar from one of the boxes. Luckily, Grandma Mimi had been visiting and retrieved the collar before Ryan could destroy it.

"I wish Mimi hadn't flown back to New

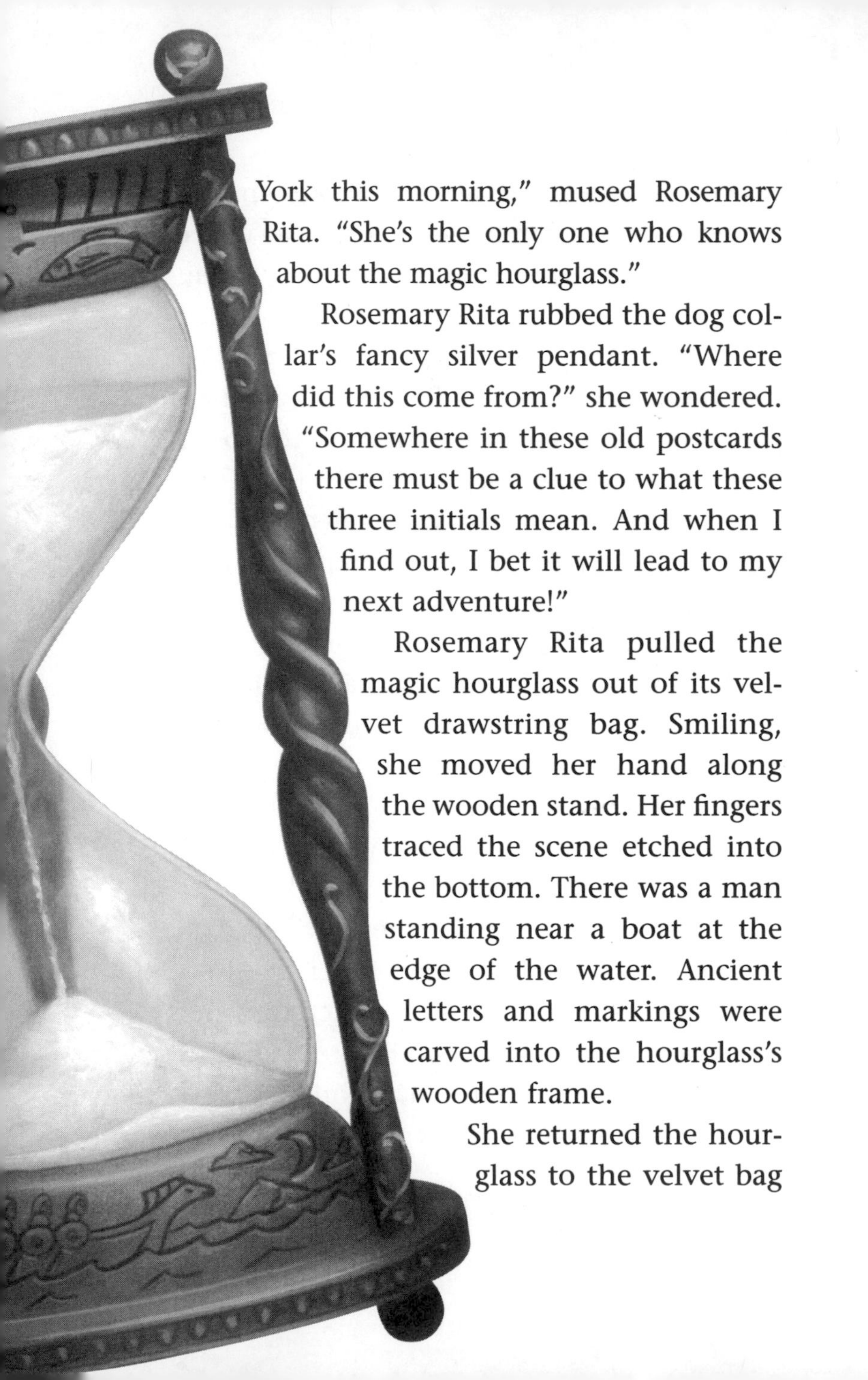

York this morning," mused Rosemary Rita. "She's the only one who knows about the magic hourglass."

Rosemary Rita rubbed the dog collar's fancy silver pendant. "Where did this come from?" she wondered. "Somewhere in these old postcards there must be a clue to what these three initials mean. And when I find out, I bet it will lead to my next adventure!"

Rosemary Rita pulled the magic hourglass out of its velvet drawstring bag. Smiling, she moved her hand along the wooden stand. Her fingers traced the scene etched into the bottom. There was a man standing near a boat at the edge of the water. Ancient letters and markings were carved into the hourglass's wooden frame.

She returned the hourglass to the velvet bag

on her lap and looked at the postcards again. Earlier, she had arranged the cards in order from the oldest to the most recent. The oldest one dated back to 1870, when postcards were first used. She searched each card for a clue about the collar, thumbing through them until she found several black-and-white ones clipped together. The front of the top postcard had a picture of a huge ocean liner with the words RMS *Mauretania*, 1919 written above it.

"That's it!" exclaimed Rosemary Rita, bouncing on the bed. She unfastened the clip and studied the cards. They were all written by Rosemary Anna Gibson, her great-grandmother, and they'd never been mailed.

Rosemary Rita read the first one, dated Saturday, September 20, 1919.

> *Dear Julie,*
> *I am terribly sad to say good-bye to London and my wonderful cousin James. He promises to write every day, but I doubt he will. The wedding was lovely. (Everything in London is called "lovely"!) James and I snuck out to the courtyard. You'll never believe what we found—an adorable Maltese puppy! It was all alone and frightened.*

James insists that I take it home to New York with me. I want a dog so very much, but Mother thinks that having a pet onboard the ship will be too much of a bother. What am I to do?

Your faithful friend,
Rosemary Anna

*

Dear Julie,
I think I'll give you these postcards in person because I missed the mail pickup. We are onboard the RMS Mauretania *now. It is so exciting. This is her first voyage with civilian passengers since the war began.*

You'll never guess who's onboard with us—my new dog, Snowball! (Like his name?)

I couldn't leave a sweet, fluffy puppy all alone in London, so I placed him in a basket, covered it with a blanket, and smuggled him onto the ship. I must be the sneakiest girl of all time. Nobody in my family suspects he is here!

Yours,
Rosemary Anna

"She never mailed the postcards. I do that too! I start postcards all the time and never send them," thought Rosemary Rita. "Wish I could make out that last sentence," she thought while holding the second postcard up to the light. As she tried to read the words that were crossed out, there was a loud crack of thunder, followed by a flash of lightning. Startled, she dropped the postcard. In an instant, the room was pitch-black. The lightning had knocked out the electricity. Rosemary Rita fumbled in the darkness for the card. After feeling around for a few moments, she found it, but as she retrieved it, the velvet bag tumbled off her lap. Rosemary Rita lunged to grab it before it fell off the bed, but as she did, the bag flipped over.

Suddenly, she felt funny—kind of light in the head. Her stomach grew queasy, as if she'd just stepped off a roller-coaster ride. Everything became blurry. She closed her eyes and fell back onto the pillows. Before she knew it, she had fallen into a deep, deep sleep.

When she awoke, she was still a little groggy. Rubbing her eyes, she looked around. A cold breeze nearly knocked her off her feet. She sniffed the air and noticed the pungent smell of salt water. "I'm not in my room anymore!" She looked out and saw the wide expanse of ocean. As she started to walk, the wooden floor began to move. "Oh, my goodness. We're moving. I'm on a ship!" thought Rosemary Rita, grabbing the brass rail to steady herself.

"Okay, don't panic. The hourglass must have flipped over when I grabbed the bag as it was falling off the bed. Everything is fine. I can just flip it back over and return to Greenville and the twenty-first century." Reaching into her green velvet bag, Rosemary Rita wrapped her fingers around the wooden hourglass. Then she let go. She couldn't do it. She was just too curious to find out exactly where and when she had landed.

She supposed it wouldn't hurt to take a look around. She wasn't going to actually stay there, but at least she could find out where she ended up this time. She'd been holding the postcards from the RMS *Mauretania,* so that must be where she landed. "Oh, brother, would Mimi have my head for this. But it *was* an accident," she reasoned.

Rosemary Rita heard the clicking sounds of shoes on the wooden deck and quickly ducked through a large white door. When it seemed safe, she opened the door a crack, just enough to peek out and see a group of ladies. One lady was wrapped in a black cape and the rest had on coats that reached to their ankles. They were all wearing white gloves and interesting hats. They whispered together in hushed tones.

"Whoa! I'd better stay in here where they can't see me. I don't think my jean skirt and T-shirt would pass in 1919. I wish I could walk around, though."

Rosemary Rita's thoughts were interrupted by a creaking sound followed by a loud thump. Someone had opened the door at the other end of the room, thrown a suitcase inside,

and then banged the door shut. From the light coming through the single porthole, Rosemary Rita could see that the room was full of trunks and luggage. "Guess I landed in the baggage room. Just my luck," said Rosemary Rita with a sigh as she slid to the floor.

Then she had a thought. "Wait a minute. Maybe the baggage room is the *perfect* place for an unprepared time traveler to land after all!" Rosemary Rita struggled to unstrap one of the trunks and quickly sorted through the clothes. "Here are some things that might fit! Please forgive me, whoever you are who owns this clothing. I promise to return it soon," she said as she pulled out a gray woolen jumper with a drop waist. She rummaged through a few more trunks and found a navy blue coat with a fur collar and a white cotton blouse. Rosemary Rita tore off her jean skirt and T-shirt and quickly dressed in the new clothes. The jumper was a little loose on her. The rounded collar of the blouse had a small stain, but it wasn't too noticeable. She smoothed the crumpled navy coat and put it on. Finally, she fixed her hair in a braid that hung down her back like a brown rope.

"Hope this will work. Boy, do I wish Mimi were here to help me find the right thing to wear," sighed Rosemary Rita, thinking back to yesterday's adventure. Mimi had helped her dress for the trip to the Paris Exposition of 1889. That had been quite an experience. She'd almost been trapped there forever! But Rosemary Rita couldn't think about that now. She heard voices outside the door, and it was time to leave quickly, before anyone found her.

Rosemary Rita wadded up her discarded clothing and stashed it under a bench, which sat against the wall. Then, clutching her velvet drawstring bag tightly in one hand, she opened the door. Rosemary Rita tried to stop the shaking in her knees as she stepped onto the deck of the RMS *Mauretania*.

Chapter 2

THE · RMS · *MAURETANIA*

THE SALTY BREEZE STUNG ROSEMARY Rita's eyes as she walked along the ship's deck. Wiping them with one hand, she firmly gripped her velvet drawstring bag with the other. It was chilly on the deck. Big, puffy clouds floated above her. She was glad to be wearing the navy coat, even though she worried the owner might spot her. Groups of people were clustered here and there on the deck, and some were reading in deck chairs, tucked snugly beneath their navy blue blankets. They looked like they were in an outdoor library. A couple of girls her age skipped by. They were wearing loosely fitting jumpers similar to the one she had found, and heavy sweaters and jackets. Rosemary Rita stared at the girls. Could one of them be her great-grandmother?

Beyond the girls, a white life preserver with large red letters on it hung on the wall next to the deck. Rosemary Rita walked closer to make out the letters. It read RMS *Mauretania*. "My guess was right! Wow!" thought Rosemary Rita. Her eyes scanned the ship, taking in all of the sights. Brass rails gleamed in the sun, and the waxed wood floors creaked as she walked along them. Sparkling white walls glistened with new paint, and sea spray tickled her skin. Rosemary Rita decided to sit down on a deck chair. She pulled the itchy blanket folded neatly at the bottom of the chair around her legs and chest.

"I think I'll definitely stay here long enough to catch a glimpse of Rosemary Anna. I *have* to see her. Then I'll go home," Rosemary Rita decided. "I know that Mimi would want to hear what her mother looked like at ten years old. I can't believe that I'm getting to meet all of the Rosemarys when they were young—great-great-great-grandmother Rosemarie, great-great-grandmother Gracie, and now great-grandmother Rosemary Anna." Rosemary Rita let out a little squeal of excitement.

Just then, a large man in a blue uniform with brass buttons down his front and gold epaulets on his shoulders sat down on the chair beside her. He wore a white hat with a shiny black brim. He had a white beard and white hair that peeked out from under his hat. His skin looked like a worn pair of red leather shoes. As he rubbed his beard, he said, "What's so amusing, young lady?"

Rosemary Rita jumped up, the blanket falling to the deck. Her fingers tightened around her velvet bag. She thought about running back to the baggage room and flipping over the hourglass to get home, but the man looked friendly enough. He leaned back in the chair with a warm smile on his face.

"Me? Are you, uh, t-talking to me?" stammered Rosemary Rita.

"Yes. I noticed you laughing. I was hoping you'd share the joke with me," the man said kindly.

"Laughing? Oh, I was thinking about something. I mean nothing. I wasn't really thinking about anything." Rosemary looked at the gentleman with pleading eyes. She wished he would leave.

"All right. You don't have to share your secret with me. I stopped because I like to meet all my passengers. I don't believe that we've had the pleasure yet. I'm Captain Whitaker. Everyone calls me Whitey. Anyway, I was looking for Ginger. Have you seen her?"

"No. I don't believe I've met Ginger."

"Haven't met Ginger? That's amazing.

Everyone knows Ginger. Ah, look, here she comes," said the captain, pointing toward the sky.

Rosemary Rita let out a shriek as a large blue-and-yellow parrot swooped down and landed on the captain's outstretched arm.

"Ginger's a parrot?" asked Rosemary Rita.

"Ginger's a parrot," the captain confirmed.

"Ginger's a parrot," squawked Ginger.

The captain and Rosemary Rita laughed. She took a deep breath and held her hand out to the captain. Her heart wasn't pounding so quickly anymore. "My name's, um, Mary. It's nice to meet you—and your fine-feathered friend."

She had gotten used to changing her first name during her adventures. It would be too coincidental to have the same name as her Rosemary ancestors, and it would be confusing, also.

"Nice to meet you, my dear," said the captain, Ginger still perched on his arm. "But I have to go now. Cheerio!"

"Nice to meet you, my dear," Ginger echoed as they moved away. "But I have to go now. Cheerio!"

Rosemary Rita was sorry to see them leave. "I can't believe I was nervous about talking to the captain. I'd better not get too friendly, though. Even with all these passengers on board, I don't want to draw attention to myself. It would be a problem if the captain asked for my ticket!" she mused.

"How am I going to find Rosemary Anna? Let me think. What did those postcards say? The only thing that really stood out was the dog. She was hiding a dog onboard the ship. What was the dog's name?" Rosemary Rita rested her chin on the palm of her left hand as she thought. She rubbed the fingers of her right hand in a circle around her temples.

"Snowball!" she exclaimed as the name popped into her head.

"Woof, woof."

She couldn't believe it. Just as she was thinking about Snowball, a small gray dog trotted up to her and started licking her heels.

"It can't be," thought Rosemary Rita as the tiny pug sniffed her knees and licked her fingers.

An elderly gray-haired woman waddled over to the dog. The woman had short legs and arms and was thick through the middle. She wore a long navy skirt, a double-strand pearl choker, and a fur wrap.

"Come back here, Precious," said the lady in a high-pitched voice with a clipped English accent. Once again, Rosemary Rita held her green velvet bag firmly in her hand, ready for a quick exit. Precious ran to the woman and sat by her side. The resemblance was unbelievable. The woman looked like a human version of her pug dog—same short legs and arms, same gray hair. Even their wrinkled faces resembled one another, except that the woman was wearing red lipstick and had a double chin that wobbled like a balloon as she patted her dog. Rosemary Rita relaxed her grip on the velvet bag. This lady was clearly as harmless as a ladybug.

"I'm sorry, dear. I hope she wasn't a bother. She loves to play," the lady said to

Rosemary Rita. Then, turning to the dog, she cooed, "Don't you wuv to play, my little pudding?"

Rosemary Rita flashed a friendly smile at the woman and replied, "Oh, no, she's no trouble at all. I love dogs. In fact, I was just looking for my friend. She has a little dog with her named Snowball."

"I haven't met a dog by that name yet. Let me ask Precious," said the lady as she leaned down to whisper in her dog's ear.

Rosemary Rita had to hold back a giggle as she watched the woman wait for a reply.

"Precious hasn't seen a dog by that name either. She'll let me know if she does," said the lady. The woman then picked up the dog and sat on a chair near her. Precious curled up into a ball on her owner's lap and drifted off to sleep.

"My name is Edna Harrington. You know, Precious took to you immediately. This dog of mine may be small, but she has a nose for people. Her nose is rarely wrong."

"Thank you, and I'm flattered. I like her, too," said Rosemary Rita, trying her best to keep a straight face.

Mrs. Harrington smiled. The wrinkles on her forehead looked like wavy spaghetti. Her light blue eyes crinkled with pleasure and almost disappeared above the creases in her cheeks.

"My name is Mary Hampton. It was very nice to meet you and Precious, but I suppose I should be going now," said Rosemary Rita, standing up.

"Oh, please stay a bit more. My Precious is all cuddled up for a nap, and I enjoy talking with you."

"Um, okay. I guess I can stay for a few more minutes."

"Splendid. You are a charming girl, Mary. And this is a magnificent ship. Isn't it exciting to be onboard such a famous ocean liner? And so posh, too." Mrs. Harrington did not pause for a reply. "Did you know that this very ship helped during the Great War? It carried many of our troops overseas. Of course, it was a shame what happened to her sister ship, the *Lusitania*."

"Yes, it was," answered Rosemary Rita, not knowing what happened to the *Lusitania* but pretending that she did.

"Such a terrible tragedy. Thank goodness nothing like that destroyed this beauty of a ship. Did you know the finest woods were collected from all parts of England to build her? I think the dining room is the most beautiful one I have ever seen. And believe me, at seventy-nine years old, I have seen my share of dining rooms. I always say, there is a reason the *Mauretania* is called the 'floating palace,'" declared Edna Harrington.

"I agree. This is the finest ship I've ever been on also," said Rosemary Rita. "Not to mention, the only one," she thought.

Mrs. Harrington shifted position beneath the sleeping dog in her lap.

"All the News That's Fit to Print."

The New York Times.

EXTRA

LUSITANIA SUNK BY A SUBMARINE, PROBABLY 1,260 DEAD;
TWICE TORPEDOED OFF IRISH COAST; SINKS IN 15 MINUTES;
CAPT. TURNER SAVED, FROHMAN AND VANDERBILT MISSING;
WASHINGTON BELIEVES THAT A GRAVE CRISIS IS AT HAND

Finally settled, she turned to Rosemary Rita and abruptly asked, "Now, tell me, with whom are you traveling?"

"Who am *I* traveling with?" repeated Rosemary Rita.

"Yes, dear."

"I'm, well, I'm traveling with my family," Rosemary Rita said quickly, trying to think up a story. "My whole family. All of us . . ." she paused, stalling for time. Then the perfect story came to her. "We are returning to New York from London. We went to London for my cousin's wedding. That's what we did." There was no reason she couldn't have been at a wedding like Rosemary Anna had.

"How lovely. And that explains your American accent. I'm here with my whole family, too. Precious, of course, and my niece and nephew as well. They're my sweet sister Edith's children. God rest her soul."

"How nice for you to be traveling with your family."

"Yes, quite. My niece and nephew are pleasant company, but sometimes they are just a bit—How do I say this properly?—well, just a bit dull. My sweet sister, Edith, tried so hard with them. But you know what they say: You can't make steak out of beefburger."

"It must be nice to have Precious here to keep you company," said Rosemary Rita, trying to shift the subject back to dogs.

"You can say that again. My darling Precious is like the child I never had. You know what they say, don't you? A dog is a man's best friend. It's certainly true in my case. No one has ever been a better friend to me, or more loyal, than my dear Precious."

"How nice for you," said Rosemary Rita. She tried to think of a way to find out about Snowball. "Is Precious allowed to stay in your cabin? Or is there a special place onboard ship where animals sleep?"

Edna Harrington's hand flew to her mouth as she gasped, "Of course she stays with me! My goodness, I would never allow her to sleep with all those other animals below the kitchen. She would be miserable."

"You're right. I'm sorry, I wasn't thinking."

"Don't worry," Mrs. Harrington sputtered. "It's just that the thought of my sweet

Precious all alone—" The old woman was so distressed, she could not continue.

Rosemary Rita mumbled another apology, then slipped away. "What a strange woman!" she thought. "She seemed nice, though, just a little too attached to her dog."

As she walked briskly along the deck, Rosemary Rita looked for an entrance to the inside of the ship. She wanted to find the room below the kitchen. It might not be good enough for Precious, but maybe Snowball could be happy there. If she could find Snowball, then she could find Rosemary Anna.

Chapter 3

Rosemary·Anna and·Snowball

ROSEMARY RITA PULLED OPEN the heavy door at the end of the deck and stepped into an elegant hallway. She paused to admire the dark wooden fluted columns that rose to meet beautifully hand-carved moldings. Enormous flower arrangements with spiky palm leaves were perched on shiny mahogany end tables. She walked through the hall into a lounge that looked as if it belonged in a beautiful castle. The chairs were upholstered in shiny silk fabric and had carved legs. Plush gray carpet with pink roses covered the floor. People were scattered around the room, talking in small groups. Attendants in starched navy uniforms buzzed about, taking orders and serving refreshments. Edna Harrington's phrase, "floating palace," immediately came to mind. That summed it up perfectly.

"I can't believe I'm seeing all this!" Rosemary Rita thought to herself. "It is more incredible than any movie or picture I've ever seen. I wish I could tell my friends about this place, but would anyone believe me?"

Rosemary Rita paused to catch a glimpse of herself in the ornate gilded mirrors that lined the wall. As she did, she saw a seven- or eight-year-old boy coming up behind her. He was wearing patched woolen knickers and a torn white shirt. She turned as he darted to the other side of the room. He was struggling to hold onto the leashes of the two dogs that he was walking, but they kept getting tangled around the table legs. Finally he yanked the leashes free, but knocked over a table in the process. Some of the other passengers turned their eyes to see what was going on. Ignoring everyone else, Rosemary Rita followed the scruffy boy as he wove around the chairs and people, through a set of glass doors.

"Slow down!" cried Rosemary Rita. "I have something to ask you."

The startled boy stopped for a moment. His big blue eyes stared at her, his eyebrows raised in an arc. "What are you after? I didn't mean to knock the table down."

Rosemary Rita blurted, "I saw you with the dogs, and I was hoping that you could show me where they keep the animals onboard. Can you, please?"

"Is that all you want? Easy. Come on, I'll take you there myself. I was going down anyway." Rosemary Rita noticed that he spoke with a thick accent. It sounded different from Mrs. Harrington's. "His accent reminds me of my friend Amanda Barnes's nanny from Ireland. I wonder if he's Irish?" thought Rosemary Rita as she followed him down a grand staircase with ornate iron railings. The thick, rounded banister felt cool

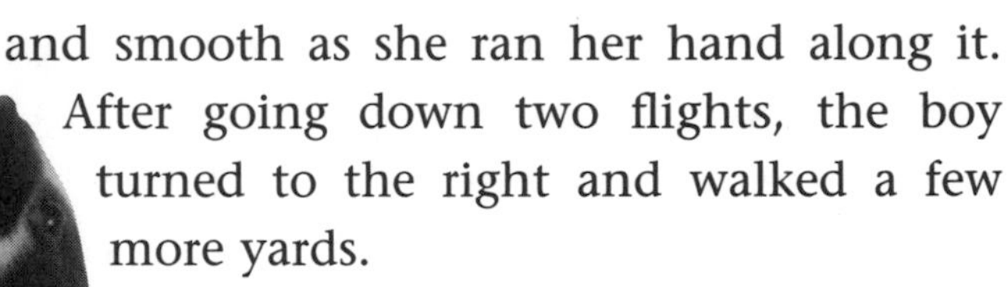

and smooth as she ran her hand along it. After going down two flights, the boy turned to the right and walked a few more yards.

"Ugh! What's that smell?" Rosemary Rita asked, holding her nose. "Guess we've found the animals."

The boy laughed. "Aw, it's not so bad. You should smell the barn at our farm. Our old farm." The boy looked distant for a moment, but he quickly recovered. "Don't know what was worse, the goats or the pigs."

Rosemary Rita laughed. "Do all of the animals onboard have to stay here?"

"Nah, there are a few lucky ones that get to sleep in the cabins in the Upper Deck. It burns my father up that those animals have it better than us."

"I agree, that doesn't seem fair," said Rosemary Rita, imagining Precious perched on a fancy pillow.

Rosemary Rita trailed behind the boy, who pulled the dogs into a room that opened up onto a deck on the other side. They were greeted by barks, meows, and squawks. The rank smell coming from the cages that lined the walls made Rosemary Rita swoon. There were animals of all shapes and sizes—dogs, cats, birds, and even a snake! Almost every cage was occupied, there were only a few empty ones at the end. "No wonder Mrs. Harrington was so upset at the thought of Precious staying here," thought Rosemary Rita.

She walked along the row of cages, peering into each one. When she reached the last

one, her heart sank. There was no sign of a small white Maltese puppy. She hadn't found Snowball, and she was no closer to finding Rosemary Anna.

"Thanks for showing me how to get here," she called to the boy in a flat voice. Putting one of his dogs in its cage, he nodded and waved good-bye.

Rosemary Rita walked out of the room with her head down and her shoulders hunched over. She let out a sigh. "There are too many people on this ship. I'll never find my great-grandmother," she moaned. Deep in thought, she turned off to the right instead of the left. As she slowly shuffled along the corridor, she tripped over a small, fluffy lump on the floor. The lump let out a squeal. Rosemary Rita screamed. The lump was a dog!

"I'm so sorry, I didn't see you," Rosemary Rita said to the little white dog. She felt like Mrs. Harrington, talking to dogs as though they were humans.

"Don't worry, you didn't hurt him," said a girl who was seated on a bench beside the dog.

The girl was dressed in a gray jumper similar to the one Rosemary Rita had found. She wore a cardigan sweater and a big white bow in her dark blond hair. Just like Rosemary Rita, she had fair skin, rosy cheeks, and green eyes with a glint of mischief in them. Rosemary Rita would recognize those green eyes anywhere. This had to be Rosemary Anna!

"Nana! It's you!" exclaimed Rosemary Rita.

"Nana?" the girl asked.

"Did I say 'Nana'? I meant Anna, Rosemary Anna. Aren't you Rosemary Anna?" Rosemary Rita's words tumbled out as she tried to cover her mistake. It had been almost two years since her great-grandmother had died. She had missed the sweet old lady who told her stories and baked her gingerbread cookies. Now she was with her Nana again! "I can't believe she was ever this young!" thought Rosemary Rita as she stared at the girl in front of her.

"How do you know my name?" asked Rosemary Rita's great-grandmother. "Most people call me May-May."

Rosemary Rita snapped back to attention. "I'm sorry. I was just excited to finally catch up with you. I'm Mary Hampton. Your cousin James pointed you out at Lydia's wedding in London, but we never got to meet. When he found out we'd be sailing on the *Mauretania* together, he insisted that I try to find you." Phew! Rosemary Rita had managed to blurt out a story that was almost believable.

Rosemary Anna smiled. Her green eyes shone with delight. "Oh, you know James? How lovely! It's nice to meet you, Mary. Any friend of James's is a friend of mine. In fact, that's how I ended up with this little guy," said Rosemary Anna, pointing at her puppy. "Did James tell you about Snowball?" she asked, bending over to pick up her small, furry pet.

"As a matter of fact, he did. That's why I came down here. James asked me to help you take care of Snowball." The words poured out of Rosemary Rita's mouth. "I can't believe that I can make up this stuff so quickly," she thought to herself. "I feel bad lying to Rosemary Anna, but there's no way that I could tell her the truth. She'd have the captain lock me up."

"That James!" exclaimed Rosemary Anna, smiling. "Well, I would love some help." She pushed a strand of her dark blond hair out of her eyes.

"Okay, May-May. Tell me, how have you kept your family from finding out about the dog?"

"It's not been easy. I keep her down here in one of the cages at night. I've become friends with the steward, and he lets me come and go as I please. During the day, I take him for walks on the Promenade Deck. My family always stays on the Upper Deck, so they don't see me. At mealtime, I stash bits of food in my napkin, then sneak out to feed him. Would you believe his favorite dish is Yorkshire pudding?" remarked May-May with a laugh.

"That's funny," chuckled Rosemary Rita.

May-May glanced at Rosemary Rita's shoes, then asked, "Are you from Holland? Those wooden shoes are so different."

"What, my clogs?—Oh, no, I forgot that I was still wearing them!—Um, they were a present," replied Rosemary Rita, praying that this would be believable.

"They're really nice. I like things that are unusual."

"Thank you. I'm so glad that I ran into you." Then, leaning down to Snowball, she said, "I didn't mean to run *over* you."

"Oh, he's fine. It was nice to see you, too. Do you have to leave so soon?" asked May-May. "I thought I'd take Snowball for a walk on the Promenade Deck. As I said before, my mother never goes there; it's much too windy for her. But it's much nicer than the Upper and the Shelter Decks, not so formal and stuffy. I also want to watch the dress rehearsal for the talent show. My sister said there will be three men dressed up as ladies!"

"Mind if I tag along? I did promise James, and—"

"That would be fun!" May-May interrupted. "Come on, let's go. The smell down here is atrocious."

"Great. I'm right behind you," replied Rosemary Rita with a big smile. She happily drifted up the red-carpeted stairs behind her great-grandmother and Snowball.

Chapter 4

Time·for·Fun

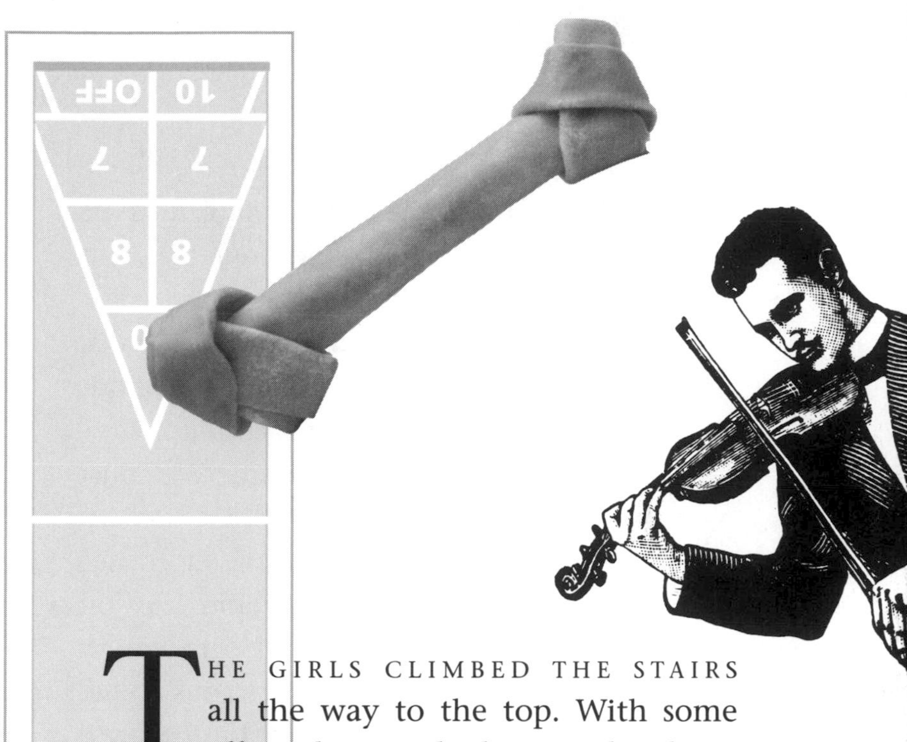

THE GIRLS CLIMBED THE STAIRS all the way to the top. With some effort they pushed open the doors leading to the Promenade Deck. The wind whipped around them, blowing their hair in their faces. They chatted away happily, as if they'd known each other forever. Snowball started straining at his leash and barking excitedly.

"What is it, Snowball?" asked May-May.

Rosemary Rita smiled. "I've never seen people talk to animals so much in my life," she thought.

Snowball's barks were answered by

another dog's. The girls let Snowball lead them along to a small, gray pug and its owner. Rosemary Rita laughed. It was Precious and Mrs. Harrington!

"Hello, dear. I see you've found your friend and her dog. My darling Precious seems to like your pet. How fortunate. Now my girl has a boyfriend onboard. We must get them together to play."

"Mrs. Harrington, I'm surprised to see you up here. I thought you would stay on the Upper Deck," said Rosemary Rita.

"Well, dear, I wanted my Precious to get a little direct sunlight, although I must say it is windy here. Then again, I'm a sturdy sort. As I always say, a little fresh air never hurt anyone." Mrs. Harrington chuckled as she spoke.

Precious and Snowball nuzzled up close to each other. Rosemary Rita introduced May-May to Mrs. Harrington. Then they all sat down on deck chairs. Mrs. Harrington pulled a red ball out of her coat pocket and tossed it to Precious. The dogs nudged the ball back and forth to each other.

"Isn't that adorable?" said May-May. "They're playing catch."

"It warms my heart," said Mrs. Harrington.

The time passed quickly as Mrs. Harrington told them all about the ship and many of the passengers. Then, checking her delicate gold wristwatch, she said, "Oh, my, I hate to break up this little party, but I have a hair appointment in a few minutes. I want to look my best for the big gala this evening."

"Do you want us to watch Precious for you?" offered Rosemary Rita.

"You're an absolute dear to offer, but I promised a young lad I'd pay him to mind her for a few hours. I think that he could use an extra quid."

Rosemary Rita thought back to the boy who had shown her the way to the kennel area. She wondered if he was the one Mrs. Harrington was referring to.

Precious whimpered as Mrs. Harrington tucked her under her arm and carried her away. The girls and Snowball walked to the other side of the Promenade Deck. It was much more crowded than the Upper Deck.

Some people were resting in deck chairs, reading books and sipping hot tea. Others were huddled in a circle playing a card game. One group was playing shuffleboard near the ship's railing. Another group was gossiping and laughing in the corner. A small band was perched at the end of the deck, playing music. Small children ran wildly from one end of the deck to the other, squealing as they squeezed by the grown-ups. Waiters were passing out cups of hot tea and sandwiches. It looked more like a big party than a gathering of passengers on a cruise ship.

"Let's stay close to each other," said Rosemary Rita. "We could get lost in all of this confusion!"

"Oh, yes. You can see why I can walk around unnoticed. My mother would never come up here. People are having too much fun for her taste. Besides, she doesn't think the cabins in second and third class are as comfortable. The Upper Deck is quite posh, you know."

"Oh, I think Gracie would like it here. She's so adventurous—"

"Gracie! You know my mother? And you call her Gracie?" May-May's eyebrows rose in disbelief.

"No, of course I don't know her. It's just that, um, James, well, he always refers to his Aunt Gracie as so much fun and everything. I guess I just *feel* that I know her." Rosemary Rita stumbled over her words as she tried to cover her mistake.

"It's true, James does get along well with Mother. It's just a little peculiar that he would talk to you about her."

"He didn't say much, really. I don't know why I brought it up. Hey, May-May, why don't we play a game of shuffleboard? Snowball can cheer us on."

"I'd like that." The girls and the puppy went over to wait for a turn at the shuffleboard game. May-May tied Snowball's leash to a nearby deck chair. A dispute had broken out between the players, and a small crowd had gathered around the playing court. A tall, lanky man with slicked-back hair was playing against his wife. Her clothes hung from her skinny body and her frizzy hair blew in her face. The woman's voice rose as she spoke to the man.

"Seymour Smedley! I won this game fair and square. You cheated," she squawked.

"I did not. You're a liar," said the man, tapping his shiny shoes on the deck.

The couple turned and noticed that a crowd had gathered. Their faces turned pink with embarrassment, and they softened their voices. "Shirley, dear, I do apologize," said Seymour. "Perhaps I was mistaken when I added up the score."

"Don't worry. It was a simple mathematical error. I take back what I said."

Now that the disagreement was settled, the spectators moved away.

The girls looked at each other. "What a strange couple!" exclaimed May-May.

"You can say that again," agreed Rosemary Rita. "Did you see the way they changed their behavior when they spotted the crowd?"

"I sure did. Look, the board is free now. Do you still want to play?"

"All right, but I'm not sure how to play," said Rosemary Rita.

The court was painted onto the deck of the ship. The triangular sections were marked with the numbers ten, eight, and seven. May-May explained the rules of the game and pointed out the penalty area. "If your disk lands there, you lose ten points." May-May used the stick to send the disks gliding down the court. She scored several points right away. Rosemary Rita lined up one of the disks and sent it hurling over the court, past May-May, where it almost slid into an old man.

"Are you trying to win the record for the longest shot hit out of bounds or for injuring the most passengers?" laughed May-May.

"Very funny," said Rosemary Rita. "I must admit, sometimes I don't know my own strength." Rosemary Rita tried again. She kept the disk in play. She was no shuffleboard whiz, but she was having fun.

While the girls played, Snowball snoozed on a deck chair.

"I'm getting hungry. I saw a platter of freshly baked gingerbread cookies by the door," said May-May. "Let's try some."

"Gingerbread cookies! I never thought we'd eat them together—" Rosemary Rita stopped herself. She swallowed the lump that was growing in her throat. She and Nana had shared dozens of gingerbread cookies. Her eyes filled with tears as she remembered. Rosemary Rita wiped them away hastily. "What I mean is, I didn't think I'd meet a friend on the ship."

May-May gave her a warm look. "I understand. I'm glad that we're friends, too. Come on, let's go."

The girls got their cookies and a glass of

lemonade each and sat down on some deck chairs. They broke off a few bits for Snowball, who gobbled them up and begged for more. The sun broke from the clouds, warming their faces. Rosemary Rita was having so much fun, she almost forgot where she'd put the velvet bag. Then she remembered that she'd tied it to the chair. She reached around, untied it, and placed it in her lap so she wouldn't lose sight of it.

"What a pretty bag," said May-May as she watched Rosemary Rita run her fingers along the velvet.

"Oh, thank you. It's my favorite. I never leave home without it." Rosemary Rita thought, "That's truer than May-May knows." Then she wondered if it was time for her to go home. She'd seen Nana and met Snowball. "I hate to leave, but I guess I'd better go," she thought.

With a sigh, she stood to say her good-byes. As she turned around, the skinny couple from the shuffleboard game nearly slammed into her. They were so deep in conversation, they barely noticed. They mumbled a quick apology and ducked into the baggage room a few yards beyond.

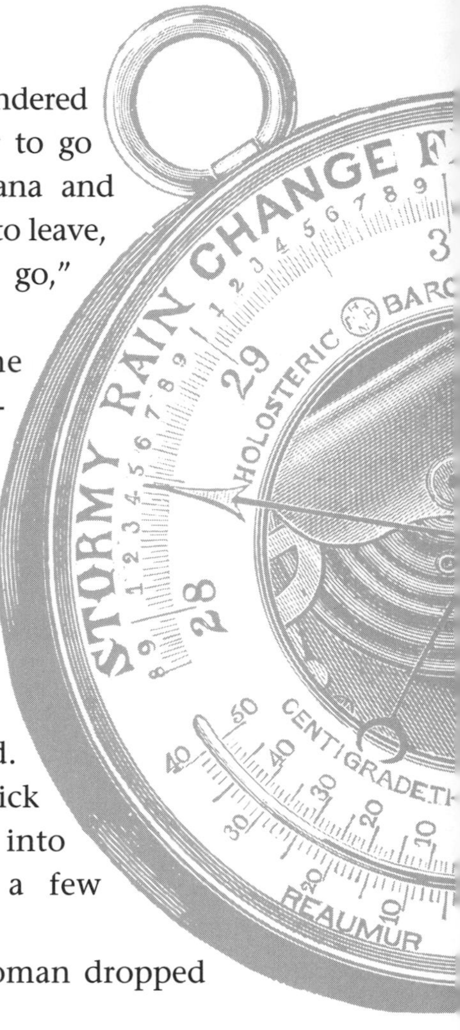

"Oh, look, the woman dropped her scarf."

The girls and Snowball walked over to the baggage room to return the scarf. As May-May was about to knock, Rosemary Rita grabbed her hand.

"Wait, what if they went in there to be alone? I don't want to interrupt."

"Let's listen for a minute and see if we can tell," suggested May-May.

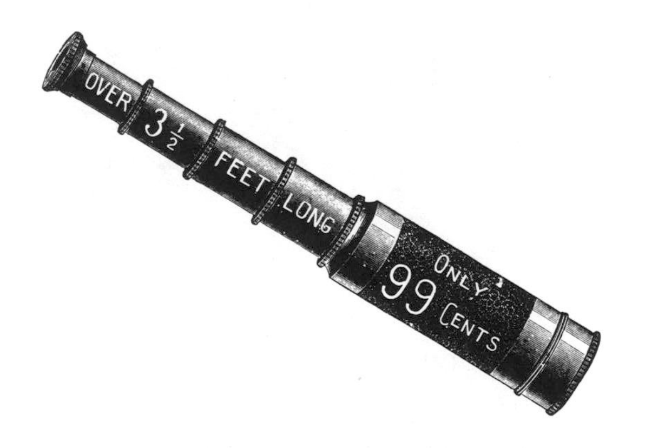

Chapter 5

A·Friend·in·Need

HUDDLED UP WITH THEIR ears to the door, the girls listened closely. Snowball let out a small bark. Both girls turned to him, saying, "Sh!" Snowball put his head down and whimpered.

"Sorry, Snowball, but we are trying to hear. Sh! We don't want the people behind the door to know we're listening," May-May whispered to her dog.

Rosemary Rita started to giggle, and put her hand over her mouth to stifle laughter. "You sound like Mrs. Harrington, talking to your dog as if he's human," she whispered.

Cat or Canine?:
If you were a pet, which one would you be? Try the quiz at winslowpress.com

"Snowball doesn't need to know *why* he must be quiet."

"Yes, he does," said May-May. Then she started laughing, too. "I didn't even *realize* I was doing it," she finally admitted in a low voice. "I guess Snowball *is* sort of human to me. The little brother I never had."

Rosemary Rita thought of Ryan crawling around in Snowball's collar. "My brother thinks he *is* a dog sometimes. If he were more like Snowball, it would be an improvement!" she said.

May-May burst into laughter all over again. "Mary, you're bonkers!" she said as she tried to contain herself.

"I know, I know," said Rosemary Rita. Then she took a closer look at Snowball's collar. It had the same brown strap as the one she'd found in the boxes, but the silver pendant was missing. "I wonder where the pendant is?" she thought.

The voices were getting louder and the girls

leaned closer to the wooden doors again.

The man's voice boomed, "She's not going to leave us anything. I just know it. We need to take the money while we can."

"Of course she'll leave us something, Seymour. Who else is she going to give it to?" The wife's voice was softer and more difficult to hear through the doors.

"Anybody. A school or a charity, perhaps."

"Oh, Seymour, don't be daft!"

Rosemary Rita and May-May exchanged glances. "I wonder who they are talking about," whispered Rosemary Rita. "Maybe one of their mothers. Who else would be leaving them money? Let's listen to what Seymour is saying."

"Shirley, we need money, and we can't wait for the old lady to die. I've lost a bundle gambling. It's only a matter of time before they make me pay up. And when I say make me, I mean by breaking every bone in my body."

"I still don't know why you gambled with those people in the first place. You knew they were crooked."

"Listen to Miss Goody-Two-Shoes. Don't get all prissy on me. I seem to remember a stack of books that disappeared from the village library while *you* were the librarian. Funny, those *same* books showed up in the boot of your car."

"All right, all right, you made your point. What's your plan? You're not going to hurt her, are you?"

"Nah, I've got a way to get the money without laying a finger on the old dame. In fact, my plan is already underway."

"Seymour, I'm not sure—"

Suddenly, Ginger flew by. Snowball began barking like mad. The girls had no choice but to leave before Snowball gave them away. They left the scarf by the door and returned to the deck chairs. May-May picked up Snowball and held him in her lap, stroking his white fur.

"May-May, what do you think of that conversation between Mr. and Mrs. Smedley? It sounds awfully fishy to me. I wonder how we can find out the old dame's name. If it's Seymour's mother, it would be easy. Her last name would be Smedley, too," said Rosemary Rita.

"But what if it's Shirley's mother? Then she'd have a different last name," said May-May.

"Well, we have to start somewhere. If we can find out the name, then we can warn the lady that she's in danger."

"It really isn't any of our business, Mary. Let's just pretend we didn't hear a thing."

"But a woman is about to be robbed of her money, and she doesn't have a clue. We *have* to help her."

"What can *we* do? Besides, I have enough trouble keeping Snowball onboard without anyone finding out. I don't need to borrow more."

"I suppose you're right. I guess I do get carried away sometimes. It's just that if we could find out . . ."

May-May sighed. "Mary, I know this is interesting, but I have something else I need to talk over with you. I was hoping that you could do me a favor. My mother and father are expecting me at a big family lunch today.

Would your family miss you if you skipped lunch? I was hoping that you could watch Snowball for me. I hate to leave him in that cage below the kitchen any more than I have to. I'll bring food back for you and Snowball, so neither of you will starve, I promise," said May-May.

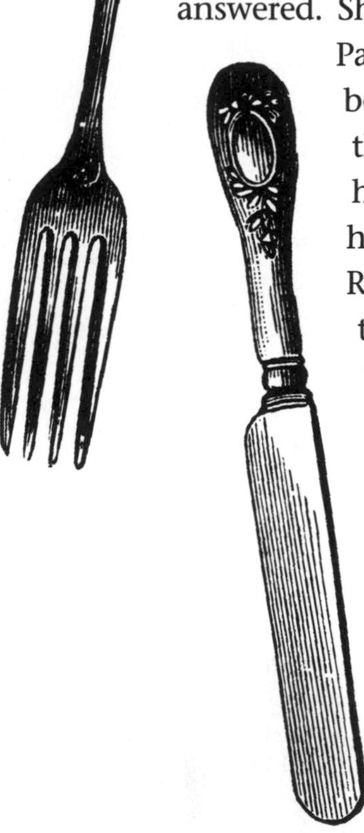

Rosemary Rita hesitated before she answered. She didn't know what to say. Part of her thought she should be getting home. But now there were several reasons for her to stay. May-May needed her help with Snowball. Plus, Rosemary Rita wanted to find the woman in danger. She was not about to ignore an adventure that was staring her in the face. How could it hurt to stay a little longer? Patting the velvet bag for reassurance, she knew she'd be fine as long as the hourglass was in reach.

"I'd be happy to help," Rosemary Rita smiled.

"You are peachy! I'll meet you by the stairs below the kitchen at two o'clock. Thank you so much. I'd better be going now," said May-May, handing Snowball over to Rosemary Rita.

R M S "MAURETANIA"

SPRING 1919

Menu

Tortue Verte   Crême Chatrillon
Supreme de Sole—Palace
Mousse de Jambon—Alexandra
Sirloin & Ribs of Beef
Green Peas   Rice   Cauliflower á la Crême
Boiled, Mashed & Chateau Potatoes
Chapon—Chipolata
Salade de Saison
Gâteau Mexicaine   Pouding Saxone
Bavarois au Chocolat   Petits Fours
Ices
Dessert
Café

CUNARD LINE

Chapter 6

Rosemary·Rita·and·Snowball Roam·the·Ship

ROSEMARY RITA AND SNOWBALL walked along the Promenade Deck. The crowd had thinned out. “I guess most people are at lunch,” thought Rosemary Rita as her stomach rumbled. Reaching in her bag, she found the Skittles and Gatorade that Mimi had put in there yesterday. She took a sip of the Gatorade. It was a little warm. She grabbed a handful of candy and popped them into her mouth one at a time. Snowball looked up at her and barked. “You hungry, too, boy? I can’t give you Skittles; they wouldn’t be good for you. We need to find a bite to eat. Come on, I’ve got an idea,” she said, leading the dog through the wooden double doors. They walked down the flight of stairs to the Shelter Deck. Rosemary Rita had smelled the bakery shop earlier when she'd passed it on the way to the animal cages.

They trotted by the pantry, the fruit storage room, and the bread room before finally arriving at the bakery. Sweeping Snowball into her arms, Rosemary Rita peered through the porthole window into the room. A large man in a white coat and a chef's hat was lifting a tray of muffins out of the oven and transferring them to a silver serving tray.

"Yum, do you smell that, Snowball?" asked Rosemary Rita, her mouth watering. "How can we get one without the cook spotting us?" Just then the cook approached the door and started to push it open. Rosemary Rita and Snowball quickly jumped back and hid in the corner. With the tray carefully balanced above his head, the cook walked down the corridor. "Now's our chance," said Rosemary Rita. Snowball started yapping, and Rosemary Rita picked him up to quiet him down as the cook turned around.

He was a large man with wisps of blond hair curling around the edge of his chef's hat. "Hello. Are you lost, young lady?" he asked.

"Um, yes—well, no. Actually, the truth is, we smelled your delicious muffins and were hoping to try one," said Rosemary Rita.

"We?" asked the cook.

"Yes, Snowball and I," she said, pointing to the white dog in her arms.

"He likes muffins?"

"Oh, he'll eat anything. His favorite dish is Yorkshire pudding."

"That's a favorite of mine, too." The chef pointed to his bulging stomach. "There aren't many dishes that are not my favorite."

Rosemary Rita chuckled. The cook smiled. "Here, you and your dog have a couple." He handed Rosemary Rita two warm muffins and went back down the corridor.

"Thank you!" said Rosemary Rita as she and Snowball gobbled up the muffins in record time. When they had finished, Snowball licked up the crumbs that had fallen on the deck. "You sure are handy to have around, buddy. My mom would love you, especially when my two-year-old brother eats. He gets about every other bite in his mouth." Rosemary Rita thought about Ryan. She pictured his face covered in ketchup. "He would really like playing with Snowball," she thought. "When I get home, I'm going to talk to Mom and Dad about getting a dog."

She grabbed his leash. "Come on, Snowball, let's have a look around." She led Snowball past the kitchen area, pantries, and food-storage rooms. They turned the corner to the other side of the ship. They passed by the captain's office. When they passed the ship's hospital, Rosemary Rita glanced in the porthole window. Three beds were lined up along the wall, but only one was being used. Rosemary Rita heard muffled sobs coming from under the sheets.

"I wonder who's crying," thought Rosemary Rita. "I guess I would be sad, too, if I had to spend my trip in the hospital." Suddenly the sheets gave a big heave and a lady in a white cotton nightgown sat up in bed. Her black hair was bluntly cut and fell squarely around her round face. Her eyes were red and swollen and her lipstick was smudged. Just then, the door swung open and knocked Rosemary Rita against the wall. A nurse with a tray of food was so surprised, she dropped the whole thing on the floor. Snowball lunged toward the food, pulling Rosemary Rita with him. He started slurping up the beef stew and pudding as fast as he could. The nurse stared at them with her eyebrows raised and her mouth wide open. "What in heaven's name is going on here?" she exclaimed.

"I'm so sorry," Rosemary Rita began. "I didn't mean to get in your way. I just wanted to see what the hospital was like. Here, I'll help you clean up."

When they were done, the nurse announced that it was time for the woman to get some rest. Rosemary Rita said good-bye and, taking Snowball's leash, left the hospital room to continue her tour of the boat. The next room they passed was the dining room. Rosemary Rita peered through the open door. The room was two stories high with a large glass-and-metal dome that stretched above it.

The tables were set with starched white linens, white-and-gold china, sparkling silver utensils, and crystal glasses. In the middle of the room, a large arrangement of spiky palm leaves reached up almost to the second story. Servers and attendants buzzed around, serving the first-class passengers. Rosemary Rita squinted as she tried to spot May-May and her family. It was so crowded, she couldn't see them.

"Hm, they sure are fancy here—even for lunch. Oh, well, Snowball, let's keep going."

She led the dog down the corridor and out to the verandah. It was a light, airy room protected by a glass roof and three glass walls. The fourth wall was open to catch the breeze from the ocean. Wicker chairs and tables were arranged in groups on the black-and-white checkered linoleum floor. More spiky palm leaves and other lush green plants stood in pots near the tables.

As Rosemary Rita was about to leave, the ship's clock chimed twice. It was two o'clock, time to meet May-May. Scooping Snowball up in her arms, Rosemary Rita fled down the stairs to the animal cages below the kitchen.

May-May was there waiting for them.

"What have you been up to?" asked May-May. "You're all out of breath."

"Snowball and I have been investigating the ship," panted Rosemary Rita. "How was your meal?"

"It was fine. I brought some Yorkshire pudding for Snowball and a muffin for you."

Rosemary Rita didn't tell May-May she'd already had a muffin. She thanked her and slipped the muffin into her bag. Even after eating the muffin, beef stew, and pudding, Snowball gobbled up the Yorkshire pudding in minutes.

Suddenly, a loud wailing sound came from the top of the stairs.

"What's that?" asked Rosemary Rita.

"I don't know."

"Listen carefully," she whispered. "Someone is crying."

The girls grabbed Snowball's leash and hurried to find out what was the matter. They ran to the top of the stairs and gasped. It was Mrs. Harrington!

Chapter 7

Precious · Is · Missing

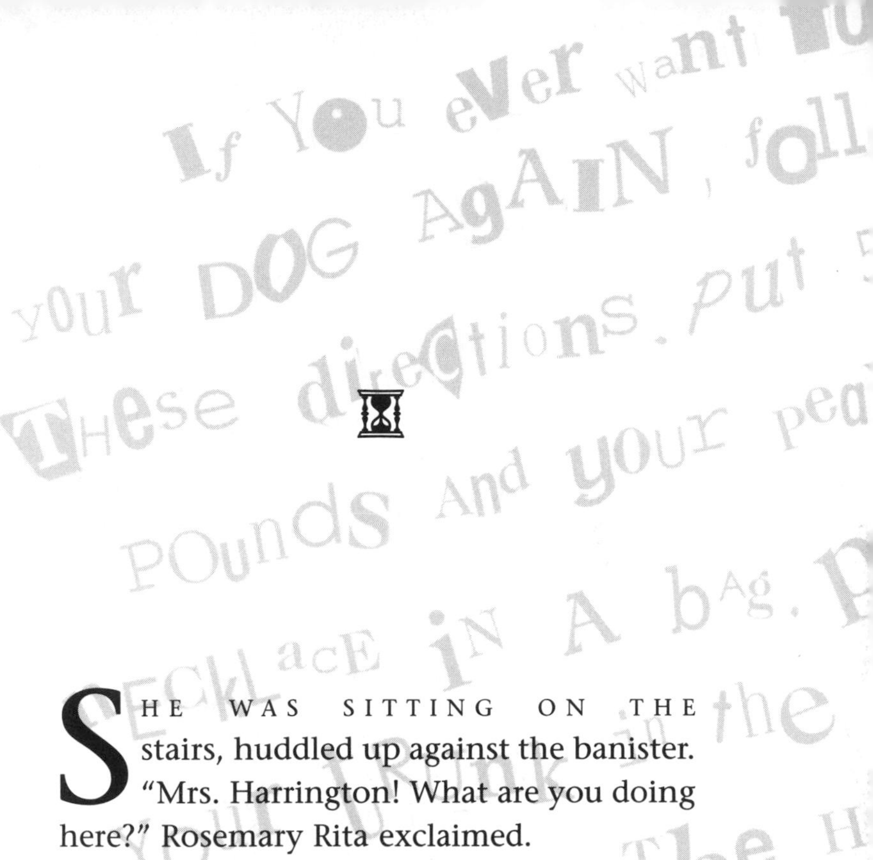

SHE WAS SITTING ON THE stairs, huddled up against the banister. "Mrs. Harrington! What are you doing here?" Rosemary Rita exclaimed.

The old woman looked up at the girls. Her eyes were red and swollen. She sniffled and blew her nose with a loud honk. "Oh, dears, it is nothing. I'm fine, now run along."

"It can't be nothing. We heard your sobs from down the stairs. Tell us, how can we help you?" asked May-May, gently patting Mrs. Harrington's shoulder.

Snowball trotted over and began to lick

Mrs. Harrington's ankles. "Where's Precious?" asked Rosemary Rita.

The old woman dissolved into loud, gulping wails. "Oh-h, my Precious. Oh-h," she moaned.

"What is it? Is she hurt?" the girls asked in unison.

Mrs. Harrington dabbed her eyes with her handkerchief, looked around, and then beckoned for the girls to come closer. "I am not supposed to tell anyone, but I don't think I can hold it in any longer. Precious is missing! Sh-sh-she's been, she's been—dog-napped!" Mrs. Harrington's shoulders shook as she cried louder than ever.

"Dognapped! What do you mean? Someone's taken Precious?" asked Rosemary Rita.

"Oh, what a shame!" exclaimed May-May.

Mrs. Harrington took several short, gasping breaths. She struggled to speak. "I-I-I can't believe my b-b-baby is gone."

"Are you sure that she was taken by someone? Maybe she's just missing," said Rosemary Rita.

Mrs. Harrington hesitated, then reached into her bag and pulled out a folded piece of paper. She motioned for the girls to come even closer. "Girls, if I show you this, you must promise not to tell anyone," Mrs. Harrington whispered as she held up the paper.

"We promise." The girls nodded, eager to see the letter.

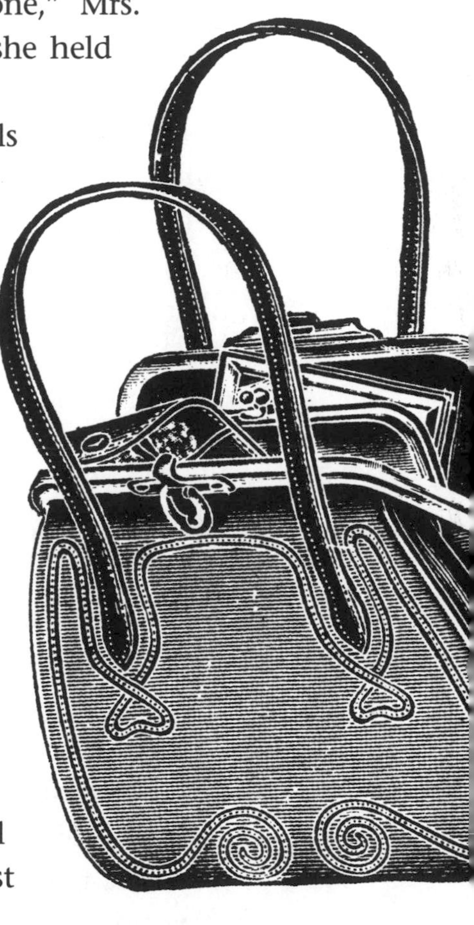

Mrs. Harrington unfolded the note. It had letters cut out from a newspaper and pasted together to form words. It was a ransom note! Rosemary Rita and May-May shrieked. Mrs. Harrington's finger flew to her mouth, "Sh!"

"I'm sorry," said May-May, patting her chest with her palm.

"I've never seen a real ransom note. It looks just

like the ones on TV," exclaimed Rosemary Rita.

"On where?" asked May-May and Mrs. Harrington.

"You've done it again!" Rosemary Rita told herself. "It looks like the ones in the Terry Vale books. I call them T.V. novels," she explained out loud. "Have you read them?"

"Never heard of them. Mary, we don't have time to talk about books now," said May-May, giving her new friend an impatient look.

"You're right, sorry. What does the ransom note say?"

Mrs. Harrington sniffled and tried to read the note. "If you ever want to see—" Then she burst into loud sobs. "I can't read it. Here, you look at it," she said, handing the note to the girls.

The note read:

If you ever want to see
your dog again, follow
these directions. Put 500
pounds and your pearl
necklace in a bag. Put it in
your trunk in the baggage
room down the hall from
your room. Do not tell
the captain or the authorities.
If you do, your dog
is going overboard!

The girls looked at each other in amazement. It was true. Precious had been dognapped!

"What are you going to do?" asked May-May.

"What else can I do? I'm going to pay the ransom," said Mrs. Harrington.

"You should go to the captain! These criminals shouldn't get away with this!" Rosemary Rita hated thieves. The idea of

Mrs. Harrington giving in to them made her blood boil.

"No! I forbid it. You read the note. If the dognappers found out, they'd throw Precious overboard. I can't chance that." Her cheeks shook like jelly at the very thought.

"Mrs. Harrington, what if you pay the ransom and they don't give Precious back?" asked Rosemary Rita.

"That's a risk I'm willing to take." Mrs. Harrington's mind was made up, and it was obvious that there was nothing they could do to change it.

"All right," said Rosemary Rita. "But when was the last time you had Precious? Maybe we can help you figure out a suspect or suspects."

"Well, just after I left you two, I took Precious to the young lad, Liam. He was watching her while I had my hair appointment, remember? When I went back to pick her up, Liam said that while his back was turned, Precious disappeared into thin air. He was holding several leads in his hands and didn't notice that one had slipped away. I returned to my room to see if she had run there, and I found the ransom note. I was so worried, I couldn't even eat lunch. I came down here to see if they had put her in one of the animal cages."

"Did you talk to Liam again?"

"Well, no. . . . He's just a lad, and he felt terrible."

"Still, he's the last one who saw her. Do you mind if May-May and I do just a little investigating? Maybe we can find out something. What's Liam's last name and where is he staying onboard?"

"His name is O'Brien, I think. Liam O'Brien. Yes, that sounds right. I'm not sure where he's staying. I only met him on the Upper Deck. I admired how he was taking such good care of Mrs. Merrill's dogs. I asked the steward to inquire if he'd like a job watching Precious. It was obvious that he could use some extra money. He was wearing a ripped shirt and dirty woolen knickers."

Rosemary Rita's hand flew to her mouth. "He sounds exactly like the boy I saw earlier. Is he about seven or eight years old?"

Mrs. Harrington nodded.

"With red hair, freckles, and kind of scruffy looking?"

"Yes, yes, that sounds like him," said Mrs. Harrington.

"It must be the same boy. Come on, May-May. Let's go find him. Mrs. Harrington, we'll report back to you in an hour. We'll meet you in your cabin; you shouldn't stay down here."

Rosemary Rita grabbed May-May by the arm. Before she had a chance to protest, Rosemary Rita whisked her down the stairs toward the third-class section of the boat. The hallway was much narrower there and the ceiling lower. A drab green carpet covered the floor. At the end of the hall, the double steel doors leading into the third-class sleeping area were propped open. May-May peered through the doors and gasped at the sight of the rows and rows of steel bunk beds. "Mary, wait," she cried. "I'm scared. I don't want to go in there."

Rosemary Rita patted her on the arm. "It will be okay, I promise. We'll just find Liam, ask him a few questions, and then leave.

These are the same people who have been walking around on the deck. You walk Snowball there all the time. It will be fine."

"All right, if you're sure," said May-May, holding tightly to Snowball.

The third-class section of the ship was very different from the elegant main cabin. People were packed like sardines into the large open room. Mothers with two and three children in their laps huddled together. There were no crystal chandeliers like the ones in the dining room. Instead, bare light bulbs dangled from the ceilings.

"Oh, this is terrible. How can they treat people like this?" thought Rosemary Rita. Liam's father was right, some of the animals had it much better than these passengers—certainly Precious did.

She spotted a kind-looking woman wearing a shawl and walked up to her. "Excuse me, ma'am. We are looking for a boy named Liam O'Brien. Do you know him?"

"O'Brien? He must be one of Seamus's children. What do you want with him?"

"He has been walking our dog. We just want to ask him a question."

"Well, their bunks are two rows over." Then, looking at May-May's frightened face, she added, "Don't be scared, now, dear. The father won't hurt you. He was only a political prisoner. People say he was falsely arrested."

At that, May-May's eyes seemed to pop out of their sockets. Before Rosemary Rita could stop her, she turned toward the exit. Rosemary Rita reached out and grabbed her arm. May-May whispered frantically, "Prisoner! The father is a convict. We have to get out of here fast."

"Okay, I'm right behind you. Do you want me to hold Snowball?"

"No, I've got him." The dog was clutched firmly in her arms. "Come on, let's go."

The girls and the dog darted up the stairs and ran down the hall to Mrs. Harrington's cabin.

"We'd better be careful. My cabin is just around the corner from Mrs. Harrington's. I don't want anyone in my family catching me with Snowball," said May-May.

"Don't worry; if they spot us, we can say that Snowball is my dog," suggested

Rosemary Rita.

"Mary, you are so clever!" She patted Rosemary Rita's arm with her free hand. "Why didn't I think of that?"

The two girls stopped in front of cabin forty-eight. Huffing and puffing, they paused to catch their breath before knocking.

Chapter 8

The·Suspects

MRS. HARRINGTON ANSWERED their knock immediately. Snowball squirmed out of May-May's arms and jumped to the floor. He barked and ran to the chair where Precious was cuddled up on a fancy pillow.

"Precious!" the girls yelled. "When did she get back?"

Mrs. Harrington was beaming with joy. "Just a few moments ago. Isn't it wonderful? My sweet, darling Precious is back with me where she belongs." She bent over and patted the dog on the head.

"That was quick. How did you manage it?"

"I paid the ransom, and the dognapper made good on his word. Within minutes of dropping off the money, I heard Precious barking outside my door. Poor little love, she was shaking like a leaf."

"What about the dognapper? We can't let him get away!" Rosemary Rita was worried, because now that the ransom was paid, they might never be able to find the culprit.

"Mary's right. We should go to the captain."

"I don't want the dognapper to get away with this any more than you do, but I'd rather not go to the captain until I have an idea who was involved."

"That's where we come in. We have found out some information that might help."

"What's that?" asked Mrs. Harrington.

"Liam's father is a convict!" blurted May-May.

"A convict?" asked Mrs. Harrington.

"Yes, and there's more. He was very resentful about how well some of the dogs were living," added Rosemary Rita.

"The father has been in prison, and *his* son was the last one seen with Precious before the dognapping."

Mrs. Harrington waved her gloved hand in the air. "Girls, I appreciate your tracking down this information for me. However, the whole thing has simply left me knackered. If you don't mind, I think I'll speak with the captain in the morning. Precious is back safe and sound, and that's all that matters. Besides, I'm ready for a celebration. My niece and nephew should be joining me any minute. We are going to have a nice glass of champagne."

Scooping up Precious in her arms, she cradled the pug like a baby. "I'll be sure to bring you the best cuts of meat, my darling Precious. Right now, you need to rest a bit."

Turning her attention back to the girls, she said, "I'm sure that I will see you at dinner. Tonight is the big gala on the ship. That's why I was getting my hair done. Oh, if only I hadn't left Precious with that convict's son, she wouldn't have had to suffer so. It does sound like the boy and the father could have been in cahoots."

There was a loud knock on the door. Mrs. Harrington waddled over to open it.

The girls gasped when the couple from the shuffleboard court walked into the room!

Rosemary Rita whispered in May-May's ear, "What are Mr. and Mrs. Skinny Minnies doing here? Why would Mrs. Harrington invite them?"

Precious leaped off the chair and ran over to the Smedleys. She ran back and forth in front of them, barking loudly at the visitors. Mrs. Harrington scooped her up. "What's the matter, pudding? You don't need to worry. It's just Seymour and Shirley." Then she turned back to her guests. "I'm sorry that she's acting like this. She's had a harrowing experience and must still be wound up."

Precious calmed down for a moment, and Mrs. Harrington introduced Seymour and Shirley Smedley to the girls.

The Smedleys looked uncomfortable, but they quickly recovered.

"Oh, what a pleasure to make your acquaintance," said Shirley.

"Yes, indeed," added Seymour. "Any friends of our dear aunt Edna are friends of ours, too."

Rosemary Rita and May-May exchanged glances.

"I can't believe they're related to Mrs. Harrington," whispered Rosemary Rita.

"I know," agreed May-May. "They're so tall and thin and she's so short and well—not thin!"

Seymour sat down next to Mrs. Harrington. Precious went wild. She snarled and barked at him. Snowball joined in the barking, too.

"Why don't we take Precious and Snowball on deck for a little walk while you have your champagne?" offered Rosemary Rita.

"Oh, no, dears, I couldn't possibly part with her so soon after getting her back," said

Mrs. Harrington. But as Precious continued to growl and carry on, Mrs. Harrington finally agreed. "Well, maybe the fresh air would do her some good. Bring her back in twenty minutes, please. Honestly, I don't know what's gotten into her. She loves visitors."

Rosemary Rita took the leash from Mrs. Harrington, and May-May grabbed Snowball. The two girls said their good-byes and left the cabin.

"This is terrible," said Rosemary Rita as they made their way down the hall and through the double doors to the deck.

"Can you believe that those two are related to sweet Mrs. Harrington? asked May-May.

"No, I can't. And there's something else that's bothering me. Did you see how Precious was acting with them?" asked Rosemary Rita.

"Precious is probably still upset from the dognapping, like Mrs. Harrington said."

"But she didn't act that way with *us*. Oh, no, I just remembered something."

"What?" asked May-May.

"How could I be so stupid?" exclaimed Rosemary Rita.

"What is it? Tell me."

"Remember the conversation we overheard? Could Mrs. Harrington be the old dame that Seymour was talking about? What if they were planning the dognapping when we overheard them talking? What a dope I am! If only we had guessed. I just assumed they were married to each other, not brother and sister. We have to figure out a way to get Mrs. Harrington's money and necklace back!" exclaimed Rosemary Rita.

"Wait a minute. What about Liam's father? He had a motive, too. Precious is living better than his family, and you know he's a convict."

"Um, that does make sense, too. Well then, we've got to find a way to draw the real dognapper or 'nappers' out."

Chapter 9

THE·PLAN

THE GIRLS PACED BACK AND forth, walking the dogs on the deck. "What should we do?" Rosemary Rita asked.

"Mrs. Harrington is going to the captain in the morning. Couldn't we just wait until then? I don't think that there's anything we can do right now," said May-May.

"I think there *is* something we can do," said Rosemary Rita confidently. "What if we confront all three suspects?"

"Confront them? Are you crazy? That would be dangerous. They might hurt us, or worse yet"— May-May's lips began to tremble—"kill us."

"We'll be fine if we act smart. I was thinking, if we let them know that we suspect them, they might try to move the necklace to a different location."

May-May looked confused. "Yes, and then what?"

"We'll follow them, get the necklace back, and bring it to Captain Whitaker. Then the captain will have the evidence to lock them up. It's not like they could get very far. We're on a ship in the middle of the ocean, after all."

"That sounds like a dangerous plan." May-May shook her head. "What would we do if they noticed us following them?" she asked.

"They won't. Anyway, *they* don't know that *we* know that *they* are the ones who took Precious," said Rosemary Rita, fumbling through her bag for a couple of pieces of paper and a pen. She scribbled some words on the papers and then showed them to May-May. "What do you think?"

May-May took one of the notes and read it:

> *Here's a warning. Tomorrow the truth will come out. Mrs. Harrington is taking the ransom note to the captain. You will be revealed as the dognapper. Better confess now.*

May-May handed the note back to Rosemary Rita. "That's pretty convincing. Hope it scares someone into confessing. Or hiding the necklace somewhere else, as you say. Just one thing: How are we going to deliver these notes?"

"I've already thought of that. You ask a steward to deliver one to Seymour at dinner. I'll give Seamus's note to the woman we met below earlier. You wait outside the entrance to the dining room so you can follow him if he leaves. I'll be posted at the entrance to the third-class section," said Rosemary Rita.

"Mary, I have another idea. Please don't think I'm a coward, but I don't feel comfortable following Seymour or Seamus. I think we should go the captain right now. He is a nice man, and I think he'll believe us. We'll tell Captain Whitaker the whole story, and then he can decide on the best way to get the necklace and the money back," said May-May.

"I guess we could do that, but how about this? We could still pass the notes out and then we can go to the captain. We don't have to follow Seymour and Seamus, if that's what's making you nervous. At least it might convince one of them to confess, even if we don't catch them with the necklace."

May-May nodded. "All right. Let's do it."

The girls walked Precious back to her cabin. Mrs. Harrington came to the door, scooped her up, and showered her with kisses. Then she thanked the girls and said good-bye. Rosemary Rita and May-May couldn't see Seymour and Shirley from the hallway, but judging from the loud barks that came from the cabin when Precious entered, they guessed the Smedleys were still there.

May-May said, "I'm too nervous to eat. Let's pretend we're not feeling well enough to go to dinner with our families. Then we can hide out in my cabin with Snowball while everyone's gone. After that, we'll go to the captain."

"That's sounds perfect," said Rosemary Rita. "I'll take Snowball with me while you talk to your parents. I'll meet you at your cabin in a half hour."

Rosemary Rita and May-May separated to deliver their notes and make excuses for dinner.

Everything went just as planned. Rosemary Rita and May-May huddled together in the cabin. "Do you think that Seamus or the Smedleys have read their notes yet?"

"I think so," answered Rosemary Rita.

"How long should we give them to do something before we go to the Captain?" asked May-May.

"Let's give them another twenty minutes, then we'll go," suggested Rosemary Rita.

May-May paced back and forth. Snowball followed behind her, barking excitedly. "Do you think that we should go now," she asked.

"It's only been a minute! May-May, you need to relax. You're getting Snowball all wound up."

"Sorry, but this waiting is killing me."

"Let's try to do something else to take our minds off it. Do you have anything in here that you like to play with?"

"I've got my jacks and paper dolls," said May-May, perking up a bit.

Rosemary Rita thought that she was too old for paper dolls, but she didn't want to hurt May-May's feelings. As it turned out, she really enjoyed playing with them.

May-May checked the clock, then asked, "Do you think we should go to the captain now?"

"All right. What should we do about Snowball? We can't take her into the dining room."

"I think we can leave her here for a little while. My family won't be back for another hour or two," said May-May.

The girls left to find the captain. When they arrived at the dining room, May-May froze. "I almost forgot. I can't go in there. My family will see me and wonder why I'm not in the cabin."

"I'll go talk to him.

My family eats in the second-story section, out of view of the captain's table." Rosemary Rita winced at having to tell another lie, but what else could she say? It was a miracle that May-May hadn't asked her too many questions about her family.

She went over to the captain's table and hovered nervously nearby. He was sitting with two elegantly dressed couples. When he saw her, he said, "Well, there's my young friend from the deck. Come, let me introduce you to the Emmets and the Lodges."

Rosemary Rita shook hands and then whispered in the captain's ear, "There's something urgent I need to tell you about."

He quickly excused himself, and they joined May-May out in the hall.

The girls told the captain the whole story, from overhearing the conversation in the baggage room, to Seamus O'Brien being an ex-con, to giving them both notes.

The captain looked worried. He shook his head and tugged at his beard. When the girls finished talking, he said, "Let's go to Mrs. Harrington's room. I would like to inspect the ransom note for clues. I'll question the suspects after I've examined all the facts."

May-May asked, "Do you mind if we stop to pick up my dog, Snowball, on the way to Mrs. Harrington's?" Captain Whitaker nodded, then ushered the girls to the first-class cabins.

Before they even reached May-May's room, they could hear loud barks from all the way down the hall. May-May ran to her cabin and hurriedly unlocked the door. Snowball bounded out of the room, running right past May-May, Rosemary Rita, and the captain.

"Where's he off to in such a hurry?" Captain Whitaker exclaimed. As they turned to follow the dog, they smelled smoke.

They ran after Snowball, who was standing in front of Mrs. Harrington's cabin, barking frantically and trotting back and forth. Smoke was billowing out from under the door.

"Run to my office and get help!" ordered Captain Whitaker. "I'll ring for the steward and see what I can do to put the fire out." Luckily, Rosemary Rita remembered having seen his office right next to the ship's hospital she'd visited earlier.

The girls ran as fast they could until they reached the captain's office and found the first mate. They all rushed back to Mrs. Harrington's room. When they arrived, they found that Captain Whitaker had managed to get the door open. He was holding Precious in his arms. Her gray fur was dirty and she was coughing, but otherwise she seemed fine. Snowball was standing close to them.

"This little dog," said the captain, pointing to Precious, "is sure lucky that your dog came to the rescue." Then he pointed at Snowball. "I kicked the door open, and the smoke was so thick, I couldn't see a thing. Your dog crawled into the room and found Precious. She was barely conscious. He prodded and nudged Precious out of the room. I've never seen anything like it. Snowball, you are a hero!"

The girls whooped and applauded. They bent down to praise Snowball and scratch him behind the ears. Then Rosemary Rita turned to the captain. "What started the fire? Do you have any idea?"

"The fire started in the bin. Someone left a burning piece of paper in there. Luckily, there wasn't too much damage. We arrived just in time. I shudder to imagine what could have happened if we hadn't come when we did."

Just then, Seymour, Shirley, and Mrs. Harrington came down the hall.

The captain wasted no time in confronting Seymour and Shirley. He told Mrs. Harrington about the conversation the girls had overheard in the baggage room. As Edna Harrington began to sob, she held Precious tightly.

"This is an outrage!" shouted Seymour.

"Lies, lies, lies!" squealed Shirley. "We had nothing to do with taking Precious or with the fire. Aunt Edna, you know we would never do anything to harm Precious."

"I'm not sure of anything right now," sobbed Mrs. Harrington.

Seymour moved closer to his aunt. Tiny beads of sweat lined his forehead. Wiping them off with his sleeve, he pleaded with his aunt to believe them.

Just then, Ginger flew into the hall and swooped down on Captain Whitaker's arm. "Take the dog, Seymour. Take the dog, Seymour," she squawked.

The captain grimaced. "So that's what Ginger was talking about? She's been saying that all afternoon. She must have witnessed you taking the dog. What do you say to that?" He pointed an accusing finger at Seymour and Shirley.

Shirley broke into tears. "It was all Seymour's idea. I didn't want to do it at all. I tried to talk him out of it, but he wouldn't listen. I love my aunt Edna. I would never try to hurt her."

Seymour's face turned a deep shade of crimson. He screamed at his sister, "How dare you try to pin the whole thing on me! You were the one who insisted on asking for the pearl necklace. You thought Mother should have left it to you instead of Aunt Edna. If it weren't for that necklace, they might never have caught us!" He was so angry, he was stamping his foot on the carpet.

Shirley covered her nose with a hanky. "We weren't going to hurt Aunt Edna or the dog. We just needed some money to settle our debts. Seymour lost a bundle of money gambling."

Aunt Edna wiped her eyes. "Why didn't you ask me for the money? I would have helped."

"Everyone knows you care more about your dog than us. We thought you were saving all of your money to leave to Precious." Seymour seemed to have calmed down, although his face was still flushed.

"That's not a bad idea. At least Precious is loyal to me, which is more than I can say for you!" replied Mrs. Harrington.

Rosemary Rita spoke up. "But why did you start the fire? I mean, you had the money and the necklace. Why did you try to hurt Precious?"

"Oh, my goodness," shrieked Shirley. "We weren't trying to hurt Precious. Seymour was only trying to burn the ransom note."

"And I guess the note wasn't completely burned when I threw it in the bin," Seymour added sheepishly.

"Oh, no!" gasped Rosemary Rita. "The other note. I better explain it to poor Seamus O'Brien. He must be pretty confused by now." She darted halfway down the hall, then stopped and ran back. She threw her arms around May-May and squeezed her tightly. "I'm so glad that I met you."

May-May chuckled. "Me, too. I'll see you in a little while."

Rosemary Rita nodded and turned away. She knew that now it was really time for her to go. Her eyes were filling with tears. She already missed her great-grandmother. "Wish that I could stay longer, wonder if I'll see her again. Maybe one day . . ." Her throat

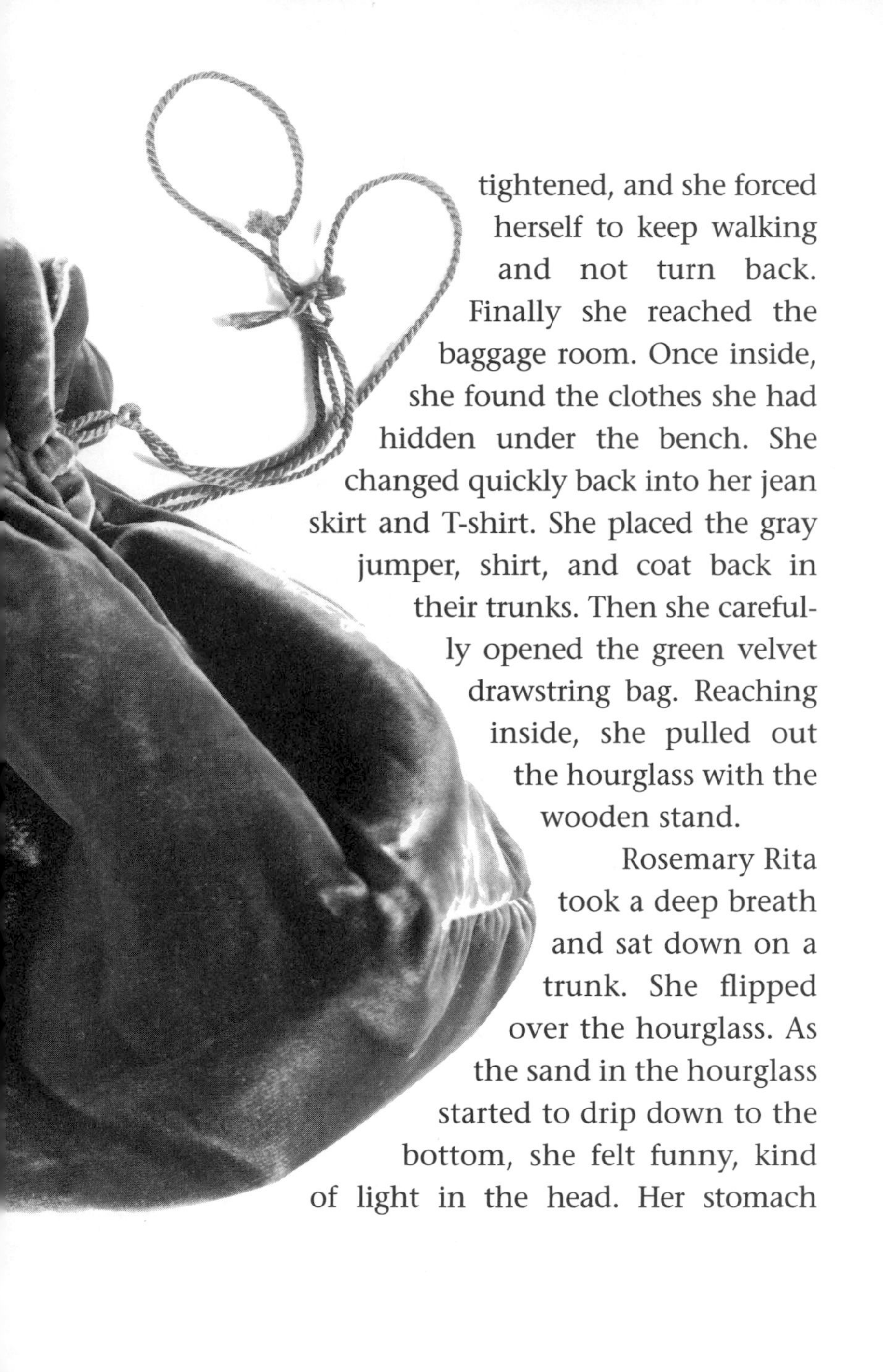

tightened, and she forced herself to keep walking and not turn back. Finally she reached the baggage room. Once inside, she found the clothes she had hidden under the bench. She changed quickly back into her jean skirt and T-shirt. She placed the gray jumper, shirt, and coat back in their trunks. Then she carefully opened the green velvet drawstring bag. Reaching inside, she pulled out the hourglass with the wooden stand.

Rosemary Rita took a deep breath and sat down on a trunk. She flipped over the hourglass. As the sand in the hourglass started to drip down to the bottom, she felt funny, kind of light in the head. Her stomach grew queasy, as if she'd just stepped off a roller-coaster ride. Suddenly, everything became blurry. She fell back against the wall. Before she knew it, she had fallen into a deep, deep sleep.

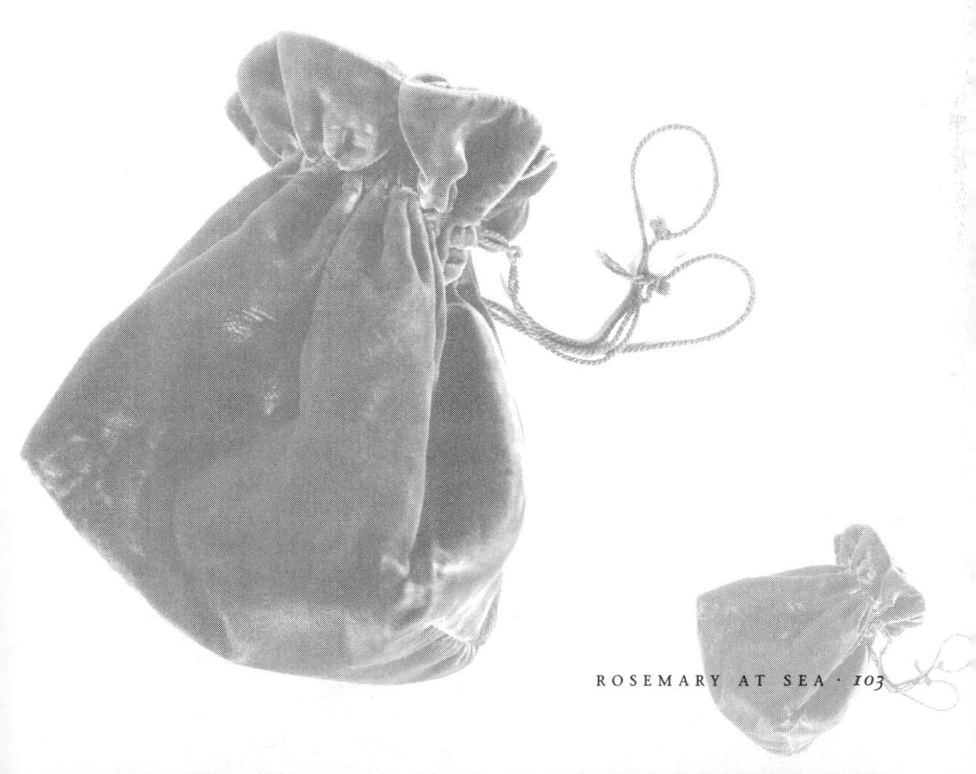

Chapter 10

Home·Again

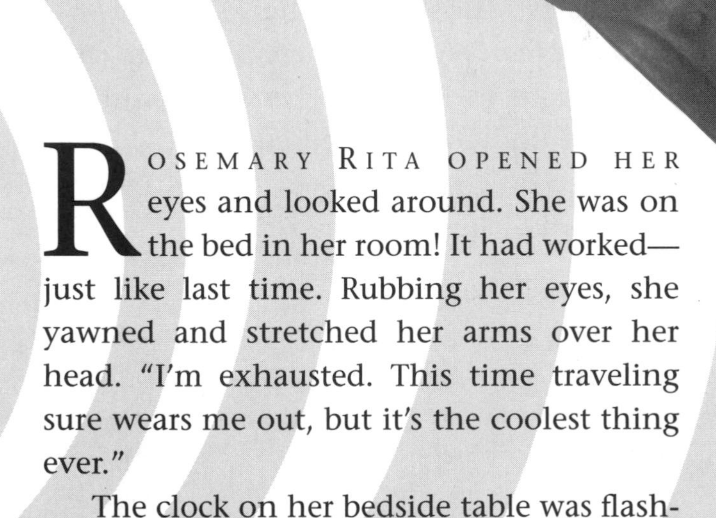

ROSEMARY RITA OPENED HER eyes and looked around. She was on the bed in her room! It had worked—just like last time. Rubbing her eyes, she yawned and stretched her arms over her head. "I'm exhausted. This time traveling sure wears me out, but it's the coolest thing ever."

The clock on her bedside table was flashing 12:00. "Oh, that's right. The electricity went out." She searched for her watch and found it. It read 8:30 PM. Only an hour had passed. "What should I do first? I guess Ryan is already asleep. I probably should find

Mom and Dad. I hope they didn't miss me," muttered Rosemary Rita. Then the pile of postcards caught her eye.

Picking them up, she remembered that she hadn't finished reading all the *Mauretania* postcards. "Maybe I'll find out what happened to Snowball," she thought. As she looked at the picture on the front of the first postcard, she smiled. "The *Mauretania*. What an incredible ship, and *I* was there to see it in person. I still can't believe it," thought Rosemary Rita as she flopped down on the bed to read the rest of the cards. The third one read:

Dear Julie,

What a day we had today. There was so much excitement! The best part is that Snowball was the hero. He saved another dog from a fire. Mother and Papa were so impressed that they agreed we could keep him. Isn't it wonderful? The captain even gave him a silver disk with the initials of the boat on it. I've fastened it to his dog collar. We are so proud of him.

We arrive in New York tomorrow.

Fondly,
Rosemary Anna

"That explains how Snowball got the dog collar with the fancy silver pendant. What a nice thing for Captain Whitaker to do. There's no mention of Seymour and Shirley. I guess that would be too long a story for the back of a postcard," thought Rosemary Rita.

She clipped the 1919 postcards back together and put them with the rest, then lay the stack on her desk. She glanced at the framed picture of her and Nana. It was taken on the Fourth of July the summer before last. Nana had a made a red, white, and blue Jell-O and Cool Whip creation. Rosemary smiled. "I'm so glad I got to see you again, Nana," she said to the picture as she laid it down. She started to walk out of her room. But in an instant, she was back. A nagging thought was going through her mind. I have been to the past and met my great-great-great grandmother, Rosemarie, then her daughter, Gracie, and now I've met my great-grandmother, Rosemary Anna. Going in order, my next adventure would be to meet Mimi when she was ten! That should be the most exciting of all."

Flipping through the postcards, she looked

for
ones from 1947, the year
that Mimi turned ten. She found five cards, and she read them all. She studied the color pictures on the front, then read them again. One card stood out among the others. It was to Mimi and it was from her father. The front of the picture showed the clearest blue water and white powdery sand that Rosemary Rita had ever seen. "Greetings from Green Turtle Cay" was printed in large letters across the picture. But it was the reference to a treasure map that caught her eye.

"This time will be different. I'm going to choose where I meet Mimi," she decided. "Now I need to see if there is a map in one of the birthday boxes." Fumbling through the boxes, she found a feather, a newspaper clipping, a broken locket, a satin ribbon, some clothes, and coins. She was about to give up when she realized there was still a box she hadn't checked. She rustled through some old newspaper articles and there, peeking out from the bottom, was what she was searching for—a treasure map! It was a yellowed and crumpled piece of paper with scratchy drawings and lots of writing and numbers.

Rosemary Rita folded the map and laid it by the postcard. Next to those two items, she carefully placed the velvet bag that held the magic hourglass. "Tomorrow, I'll set out on my search for the hidden treasure with none other than my very own grandmother, Mimi, at age ten! I can't wait."

Rosemary Rita ran down the stairs to say good-night to her parents. The sooner she went to bed, the sooner she would wake up, and her next adventure would begin.

A Note from the Author

THE RMS *MAURETANIA*

During the time that this Rosemary Rita adventure takes place, luxurious ocean liners were crossing the North Atlantic seas. The *Mauretania* was considered the largest and fastest liner of her time.

It was built after the British government voted to give the Cunard Company 2.6 million pounds (about 3.7 million dollars) toward the creation of two new super-liners. The British wanted to win back from the Germans the Blue Riband, the award given to the ship that made the fastest transatlantic crossing. The *Mauretania* and her sister ship, the *Lusitania,* were the result. They were to be the first passenger ships with the new steam turbine engine that had recently been developed by an engineer named Charles Parsons.

On November 16, 1907, the *Mauretania* made its first voyage from Liverpool, England, to New York City. Despite severe storms, she crossed the Atlantic Ocean in good time, and arrived on November 22. In April of 1909, she captured the Blue Riband with a speed of 23.69 knots. She would hold on to the Blue Riband for twenty years.

World War I began in 1914, and a year later the British government seized the *Mauretania* and painted it gray. She was used as both a troop ship and a hospital ship. The *Lusitania*, sadly, did not survive the war, as it was torpedoed and sunk in May 1915. By 1919, the war had ended and the *Mauretania* was returned to the Cunard line. She was restored to the beautiful "floating palace" that she had been before the war. It was this "floating palace" that Rosemary Rita would enjoy later that year in this story.

LIFE AND ACTIVITIES ABOARD THE *MAURETANIA*

The *Mauretania* could hold more than 2,300 passengers. Over half of these passengers traveled in third, or steerage class, a far cry from the luxurious surroundings that Mrs. Harrington and Rosemary Anna's family were in. A third-class ticket on the *Mauretania* cost only six or seven pounds (about eight or nine dollars), compared to almost 200

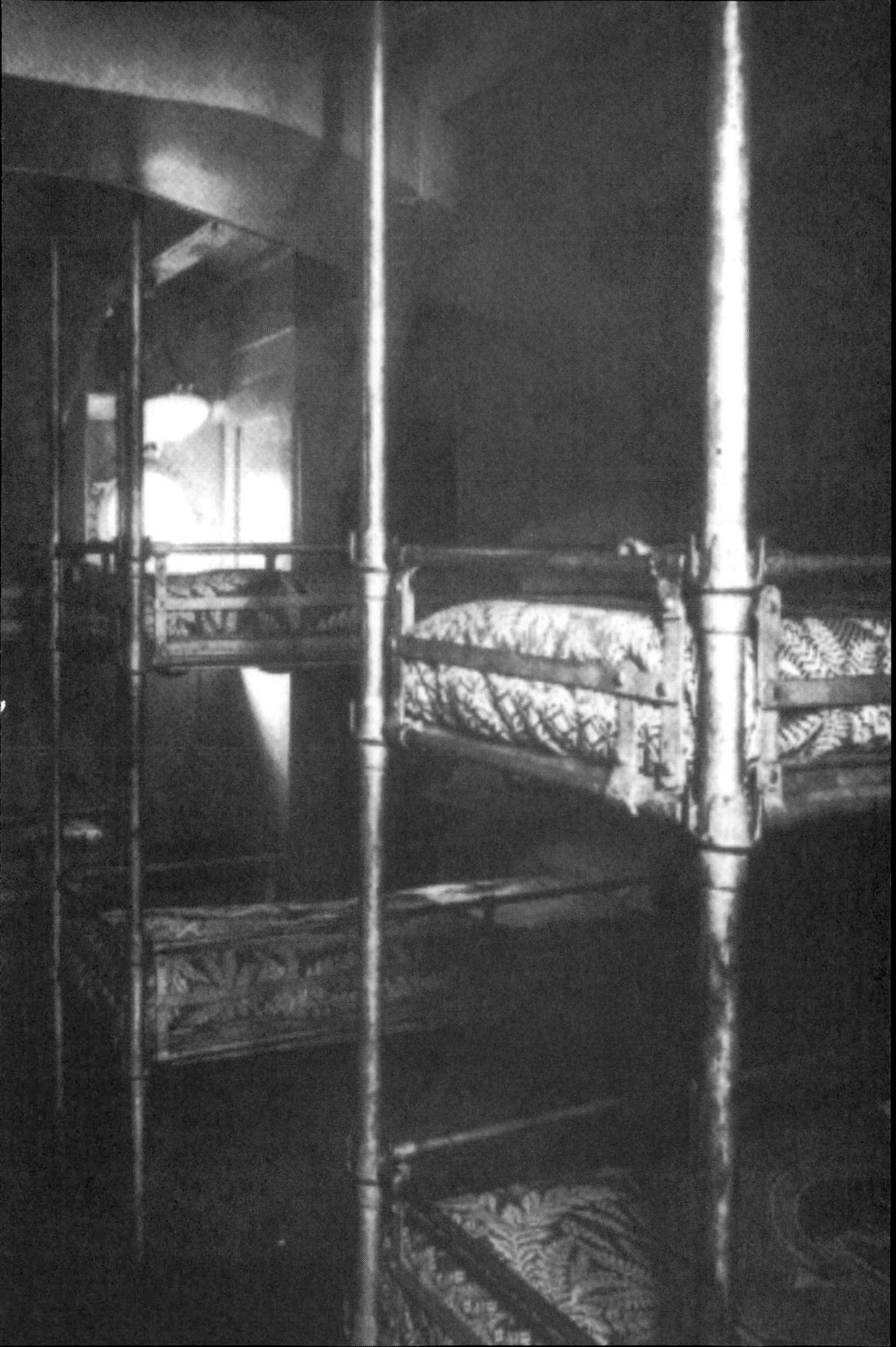

Saloon Rates S. S. "MAURE

TO OR FROM LIVERPOOL OR LONDON.

EASTBOUND / WESTBOUND	OUT OF SEASON. Aug. 16 to Mch. 31 / Nov. 1 to Mch. 31				INTERMEDIATE Apl. 1 to A / July 16 to A / Apr. 1 to Ju / Oct. 16 to O		
	L'pool Q't'wn Lond'n or Paris	Two Passengers in a room			L'pool Q't'wn Lond'n or Paris	Tw Passe in a r	
A—DECK.	Room alone	L'pool or Q't'wn	London	Paris	Room alone	L'pool or Q't'wn	Lo d
OUTSIDE ROOMS—							
*A 22, A 23, with private toilet & bath	$400	$450	$450	$450	$550	$600	$6
*A 7, 10, 16, 17	300	350	350	350	425	475	4
*A 31, 32.	250	300	300	300	400	450	4
*A 18, 19, 20, 21	250	300	300	300	350	400	4
INSIDE ROOMS—							
*A 5, 8, 9, 12, 24, 25.	250	300	300	300	300	350	3
OUTSIDE ROOMS—		Each	Each	Each		Each	Ea
A 2	200	M	M	M	275	165	1
A 3, 6	250	140	140	M	300	170	1
INSIDE ROOMS—							
A 1, 4, 26, 27, 28 29, 30,	175	M	M	M	210	140	1
A 11, 33, 34	150	M	M	M	200	140	1
	Single Berth Rooms				Single Berth		
INSIDE—A 14, 15	M	..	..	..	150	..	.
*No Single Berths will be sold in these rooms							

B—DECK.	One or Two Passengers $1250	One or T Passenge $1625
OUTSIDE ROOMS— Regal Suites— *B 47, 49, 51 & 53; *B 48, 50, 52 & 54 (Comprising 2 Bedrooms, Drawing Room, Dining Room, Private Bath and Toilet.)		

(DECK B CONTINUED.)	L'pool Q't'wn Lond'n or Paris	Two Passengers in a room			L'pool Q't'wn Lond'n or Paris	T Passe in a	
	Room alone	L'pool or Q't'wn	London	Paris	Room alone	L'pool or Q't'wn	Lo d
OUTSIDE ROOMS—							
Parlor Suites—							
*B 65 & 67, 68 & 70; *B 5 & 77, 76 & 78; *B 85 & 87, 86 & 88 (Comprising Bedroom and Sitting Room, with Private Bath and Toilet.)	$550	$625	$625	$625	$850	$935	9
*B 89, 90, 91, 92.	300	350	350	350	400	475	4
B 5, 6, 11, 12, with private toilet & bath	400	450	450	450	550	600	6
		Each	Each	Each		Each	Ea
B 18, 19, 21, 22, 25, 26, 29, 30, 33; B 34, 37, 38, 43, 44, 73, 74,	300	175	175	175	375	210	2
B 5, 6, 11, 12, without bath	300	175	175	175	375	210	2
B 104, 105, 109, 110	250	150	150	150	350	200	2
INSIDE ROOMS—							

pounds, or 283 dollars for a first-class ticket! In second class, where the average traveler would stay, the price was about ten pounds (about fourteen dollars). The rich décor and beautiful paneling and furniture of the first class were not present in the second- or third-class cabins.

An unfortunate but popular activity for some first-class passengers was called "slumming." Elegantly dressed upper-class passengers would explore the third-class quarters, often flaunting their wealth to the many poor, emigrant passengers. Author Robert Louis Stevenson recalls a particular instance of first-class passengers "slumming" in steerage class, where he himself was traveling:

> Their eyes searched us all over for tatters and incongruities, a laugh ready at their lips; but they were too well-mannered to indulge it in our hearing. Wait a bit, till they were back in the saloon, then hear how wittily they would depict the manners of the steerage.

Children in first class had their own dining and nursery area aboard the *Mauretania*. The room had red carpeting and white walls, on which panels were arranged illustrating the nursery rhyme "Four and Twenty Blackbirds." The adults, meanwhile, could enjoy a beautiful two-story dining saloon with a giant domed ceiling decorated with the signs of the zodiac. They could also dine in the Verandah café, which featured an open wall that allowed the fresh sea air to blow in and refresh the diners. Occasionally they would have invited their older children to join them.

Passengers had numerous ways to pass the time while aboard the ship. Sports, of course, were very popular. Shuffleboard was a favorite, as was deck tennis, played without rackets or balls. Instead, players used *quoits*, which were flat rings made out of rope. They were flung back and forth over the net by hand. Many people also got their exercise by walking several times around the Promenade Deck. There was a steady war waged between those who walked and those who rested in the deck chairs that often blocked the walkers.

Other shipboard activities included a mas-

querade party, which drew great interest and took hours of preparation. There were contests to determine the best costume. Generally, the men who won these competitions dressed up as women, which was considered a great joke.

Gambling was a large part of ocean-liner life. Often, someone on the ship would start a pool, collecting money from passengers who would bet money on how many miles the ship had traveled the previous day. At noon, the ship's whistle would sound, and the passengers who had entered the pool would rush to hear how many miles had been covered in the last twenty-four hours. The person who guessed correctly would win all the money in the pool. Sometimes hundreds or even thousands of dollars could be won!

Con men, or boatmen, as they were called, would prey on the more naïve passengers of first class, as Seymour would quickly learn. There were a variety of ways to swindle people out of their money on the ship. Sometimes the boatmen would make friends with a rich male passenger and persuade him to sit in on a card game. After allowing the rich passenger to win the first few hands, the boatmen would encourage him to drink alcohol. Eventually, the boatmen would swindle him out of large amounts of money. There were signs posted all around the ship telling passengers not to play poker with strangers. These signs were often ignored, leading to embarrassing and costly encounters.

END OF AN ERA

In July of 1929, the *Mauretania* lost the Blue Riband for the first time in twenty years. It was obvious that the newer liners being built were both speedier and fancier. Starting in 1932, the *Mauretania* made cruises mostly in the Mediterranean. In the spring of 1935, after years of reliable and luxurious service, she was sold to scrappers in Scotland. Thousands of people gathered at the Tyne, where she was originally built, to bid their farewell. The *Mauretania* fired rockets from her bridge and then, after everyone sang "Auld Lang Syne," the "Grand Old Lady of the Atlantic" sailed to Scotland to be scrapped.

British Words and Expressions Used in This Book

Too much of a bother	Too much trouble
Cheerio!	Good-bye!
posh	luxurious
holiday	vacation
How lovely!	How nice!
peevish	ill-tempered
beefburger	hamburger
lad	boy
quid	one pound (about $1.50)
You're bonkers!	You're crazy!
daft	stupid
boot	car trunk
peachy	wonderful
Oh, bother!	Oh, darn!
I can't chance that.	I can't take that risk.
clever	smart
knackered	worn out
dodgy	tricky
bin	garbage can
lead	leash
smashing	great

Other Useful Expressions

Cheers!	Good-bye! *(informal)*
flat	apartment
lift	elevator
torch	flashlight
Within an ace of ...	Very near to ...
carry the can	take the blame
know the score	to be well-informed about something
dilly-dally	to waste time
in apple-pie order	in good order

Generations

Rosemary Ruth "Rosemarie" Berger (Christianson)
Great-great-great-grandmother

Rosemary Grace "Gracie" Christianson (Gibson)
Great-great-grandmother

Rosemary Anna Gibson (Ryan)
Great-grandmother

Rosemary Regina "Mimi" Ryan (Carlisle)
Grandmother

Rosemary "Leigh" Carlisle (Hampton)
Mother

Rosemary Rita Hampton

of Rosemarys

BORN	AGE 10
1860	1870
1879	1889
1909	1919
1937	1947
1965	1975
1991	2001

About the Author

Photo: Kay Roper

I have wished many times over the years that my children could have known my grandmother, Mimi. I am thrilled that her spirit comes to life in these books. Now I can share Mimi with my own children and many other children as well.

—BARBARA ROBERTSON

Barbara Robertson lives in Greenville, South Carolina, with her husband, Marsh, and their three children, Ashley, Will, and Eileen. She has earned B.A. and M.A. degrees in Elementary and Early Childhood Education. A former teacher, Barbara enjoys volunteering at her children's schools. In addition, she serves on several community boards (Children's Hospital, Friends of the Greenville Zoo, and the South Carolina Children's Theatre). When she's not pounding on her word processor or chauffeuring her children, you might find Barbara on the tennis court or curled up with a good book.

WHAT'S NEXT?

Read a chapter from Rosemary Rita's next adventure at winslowpress.com